DUEL OF THE OUTLAWS

The inhabitants of Twin Pines, Arizona lead uneventful, happy lives — until the sudden arrival of Black Yankee and his gang. They shoot the sheriff, take over the place, and Twin Pines spirals downwards into an outlaw town, with lawlessness and sudden death the norm. When Thorn Tanworth, son of the sheriff, returns from his travels, to everyone's astonishment he establishes a mutually beneficial partnership with Black Yankee. But then the two men begin fighting each other for control of the town . . .

Books by John Russell Fearn
in the Linford Western Library:

NAVAJO VENGEANCE
MERRIDEW FOLLOWS THE TRAIL
THUNDER VALLEY
HELL'S ACRES
FIRES OF VENGEANCE

JOHN RUSSELL FEARN

DUEL OF THE OUTLAWS

Complete and Unabridged

LINFORD
Leicester

First published in Great Britain in 1949
as
Six Guns Shoot to Kill
by Hank Carson

First Linford Edition
published 2016

*A catalogue record for this book is available
from the British Library.*

ISBN 978–1–4448–2680–7

Published by
F. A. Thorpe (Publishing)
Anstey, Leicestershire

Set by Words & Graphics Ltd.
Anstey, Leicestershire
Printed and bound in Great Britain by
T. J. International Ltd., Padstow, Cornwall

This book is printed on acid-free paper

1

'Well, boys, I reckon this is it. Couldn't be anythin' that'd suit us better. Sort of dump where even a corpse'd be thought a disturbance.'

The big fellow on the sorrel grinned crookedly, leaned more lazily on the saddle horn, and contemplated the view spread in the misty evening light at the base of the sloping valley side. Behind him five men squatted on their uneasily moving horses, glancing at each other and nodding.

None of them were remarkable for their looks, unless considered from the aspect of ugliness. They were swarthy, burned deep brown with the pitiless Arizona sun, and their rough shirts and riding pants bore the marks of hard riding and tough living. Outlaws, each and every one of them, driven from the neighbouring state and seeking a quiet backwater in which to settle.

'And now we've found it,' the big fellow said, voicing all their thoughts. 'We can soon turn these mugs to our way of thinkin'. Never met a guy — or a dame either — who didn't see reason at the wrong end of the hardware.'

The big fellow — self-appointed leader of the band — had been christened Abraham Dodd by his hopeful parents. Now he called himself 'Black Yankee' and his unlovely features graced every reward dodger on every post and log cabin wall within fifty miles. He was a murderer, a thief, a throwback to the days when the West had been really renegade.

'No reason why we should stop up here like blasted angels,' he commented, spitting into the arid dust. 'Let's be teachin' these mugs down here that we mean business.'

He spurred his horse forward and his men followed suit. Followed by feathers of choking dust they swept down the valley's sloping side, the sprawling, cockeyed little town of Twin Pines sweeping ever nearer to them.

In Twin Pines nothing had ever happened throughout its history. People were born here, became cattle dealers, store-keepers, fruit exporters, or ranchers — married, had children, sizzled in the sunlight, kept themselves warm in the winter, and then died. Nothing more interesting than that. In many ways Twin Pines was isolated, lost to the world, flanked by the mesa on one side and the mighty Catalinas on the other. The place was not even marked on the map — and nobody knew it better than Black Yankee, fugitive from justice.

There was still considerable daylight left when Black Yankee raced his boys into the town's main street, all of them firing their revolvers noisily in the air and causing the drifting inhabitants to scuttle like the inmates of an overturned ant-hill. In the middle of the main street Black Yankee dragged his pitching horse to a halt and, with his

3

guns still levelled, looked about him at the boardwalks where the demoralized men and women were crouched and wondering.

'Hey, you mugs!' Black Yankee's voice carried from one end of the street to the other. 'Who's the sheriff around here?' Fetch him out pronto — or do I have to go gunnin' for the jigger?'

A little further up the street a tall, slope-shouldered man wearing cross-over belts emerged from the general press of people and stepped easily from the boardwalk to the dust of the main street. He was perhaps sixty, long-jawed, an uncompromising firmness in his lean face.

'I am,' he said, stopping at a distance of perhaps ten yards. 'And you're Black Yankee. I've a picture of you in my office.'

'Well, ain't that nice,' the outlaw commented sourly. 'Like all the rest of the polecats you're after me, huh? So happen I got here first, see — Get your mitts up!'

4

Sheriff Tanworth hesitated and then slowly obeyed, keeping his hands at shoulder level. Black Yankee eyed him narrowly.

'Tell you what I'm figurin' on doin', Sheriff,' he said, and glanced about him to make sure everybody was listening. 'I'm takin' this town over. Me an' my boys need a quiet place where nobody's likely to come gunnin' for us. I don't have to tell you, I reckon, that th' law'd be mighty glad to catch up on us.'

'A good thing when it does,' Sheriff Tanworth said quietly.

'You think so, do yuh? Don't start a-talkin' outa turn, feller! As I was sayin' — in th' old days, when things were worth havin' round these parts, there used to be outlaw towns — towns where no law existed — where guys, and dames too, on the run from the law were the only people in the place. Just one big hide-out. Get it?'

The sheriff's eyes narrowed. 'What's the idea, Yankee? You hankerin' after taking over Twin Pines an' makin' it an outlaw town?'

'Y'catch on quick,' the outlaw retorted. 'That's *just* what I'm aimin' to do. You get kinda sick of roamin' around the desert lookin' for a place to hide ... 'Fore I go any further, though, I've a question to ask. You got a gal in this town by the name of Claire Henderson?'

'Yeah — sure.' It was a man in a black suit and wearing a shoestring tie who answered. He was standing on the boardwalk, elbows leaning on the rail, gazing into the street upon the outlaws.

'Who are you?' Black Yankee snapped, wheeling on him.

'Steve Bradshaw. I own the Lucky Horseshoe down the street. The gal you're talkin' about works for me — hostess. She blew into town about three weeks ago ... Nice kid,' Steve Bradshaw added reflectively.

'For a murderess,' Black Yankee said ambiguously; then he turned back to the sheriff. 'We shan't be needin' you any more, Sheriff,' he said briefly. 'Jus' the same nobody'll be able to say which of us shot you. All fire at once, see?'

Before Sheriff Tanworth had a chance to move or even make a grab at his guns Black Yankee and his cohorts fired simultaneously. Then the outlaw sat watching, cordite fumes circling round his nostrils, as the sheriff crumpled slowly into the dust.

'Why, you dirty murderers!' Steve Bradshaw whipped out his .45 but before he could level it Black Yankee fired alone. The gun dropped from Bradshaw's fingers. With a contorted face he toppled over the boardwalk rail and crashed into the dirt.

'I reckon that'll show you mugs that I'm not kiddin',' the outlaw snapped. 'Get it into your thick heads that I'm takin' this town over — an' anybody who doesn't like it'll be removed pronto. Lefty — look these guys over. See if they're dead.'

One of the men slipped from his horse and examined the sheriff and saloon owner quickly, each in turn. When he had finished he stood pointing his thumbs downward significantly and grinning. Black Yankee nodded, his pale grey eyes studying the silent, appalled populace looking on.

'Shove the stiffs on your horse, Lefty, an' take 'em out to the mesa. Dump 'em there and come back. I reckon the sun'll do the rest. Ain't likely to be found there — an' if they are we'll deal with it. Get movin'!'

Lefty began to carry out the orders and Black Yankee slid from his horse. Still with his guns ready and his killer's eyes watching the men and women on the boardwalk in the fading light, he walked over to the sheriff and tore the star badge from his shirt. Then with it in his hand he looked about him.

'I reckon there's some sort of law around here,' he said, and spat casually to show his contempt. 'Might as well conform to it. Which of you white-livered skunks is the mayor of this dump?'

After an interval, during which time Lefty transferred the corpses to his horse, a stout man of unusual shortness came waddling down the steps into the street. Six-foot-three Black Yankee stood eyeing him contemptuously as he came up.

'So you're the mayor, huh? Not much of you, I reckon.'

'Not much of the town,' the mayor responded, with a rather uneasy grin.

'Don't get funny with me, feller; ain't healthy,' the outlaw warned him. 'Here — take this an' swear me in. Might as well have everythin' nice an' legal.'

The mayor found the star badge thrust into his hand. He took it, studied it, and then watched Lefty leading his horse along the main street with the bodies of the dead sheriff and saloon owner upon it.

'Get on with it!' Black Yankee roared. 'What in hell are you waitin' fur?'

The outlaw's right-hand gun prodded the mayor in the paunch and he gave a start. Mechanically he muttered the words of the sheriff's oath and then pinned the badge on Black Yankee's shirt. The outlaw glanced down at it and grinned cynically.

'Okay, that settles that, I reckon. You folks've got yourself a new sheriff — an' that bein' so I'll tell you a few things. From now on me an' my boys are runnin' this town — an' anybody who comes nosin' in lookin' fur us'll be shot out of hand. We aim to stay here an' be comfortable — an' we shan't interfere with any of you if you play ball with us. But get this — ' He paused menacingly and turned slowly to survey the faces in the twilight. 'If any of you plugs me — as you might think of doin' — my boys'll get you. You can't get all of us at once; there'll always be some left to take revenge. Just keep quiet an' nothin'll happen. Got that?'

Nobody answered. There was simply a great, menacing calm. Black Yankee completed a revolution on his heel and then put his guns slowly into their holsters, and waited. People stirred but nobody attempted to fire.

'Okay,' the outlaw said. 'That's how it's goin' to be. Jeff — stable the horses in the town livery and then join me in the Lucky Horseshoe. Rest of you boys come with me.'

He turned, three of his men following, and with arrogant strides led the way down the street to the main saloon. He pushed open the batwings and strode inside. There was a fair scattering of men and women present, but they had the appearance of having been either at the saloon's doors or windows. Certainly there seemed little doubt from their expressions that they knew exactly what had been going on.

Black Yankee paused for a moment and looked round on them, his powerful face with its hooked nose and cleft chin decidedly grim, then he turned and headed for the bar. The barkeep looked at him expectantly as he polished glasses.

'Double whiskey,' the outlaw snapped. 'An' if you think you'll get paid for it you're loco. Hurry it up!'

Because he could do nothing else, the barkeep obeyed — and he had to provide similar drinks for the outlaw's three cohorts. In silence, their elbows on the edge of the bar counter, they stood considering the men and women at the tables and draining their glasses slowly.

The immediate excitement having died down, and finding they were not being interfered with — nor, apparently, were likely to be — the men and women were continuing their normal pursuits. Mainly they were concerned with drinking or smoking. The air was blue with a dense tobacco haze through which the swinging oil lamps had taken unto themselves haloes. In the further distances the faro and roulette tables were busy. In odd corners poker games were in progress. To one side of the big saloon a three-piece 'orchestra' was doing its best to dispense tin-panny music from a battered-looking rostrum. In the midst of the people a girl was moving — slender, in a backless, sleeveless evening gown, its sequins catching the light. Black Yankee stood watching her narrowly through the haze.

'That's the dame,' he murmured finally, and plonked down his glass for it to be refilled.

'Mind if I ask you somethin', boss?' one of his men enquired.

'Ask all you want — I don't have t' answer if I don't want.'

'I was just wonderin'. You come here so's we could keep out of the way of the law? — or because of that gal over there?'

Black Yankee took up his glass, swallowed some more whiskey, and then grinned.

'Both,' he responded. 'That gal told me she was headin' for Twin Pines 'cos it was a quiet place — so I came here for the same reason. And 'cos she interests me. I think she an' me could go places . . . in a big way.'

The other man said nothing. He

glanced at his two companions significantly, and then towards the batwings as their two other comrades came in — Lefty and Jeff — guns in the crossover belts slapping against their thighs. All of them were aware how Black Yankee had first come in contact with the girl. It had been in the hundred-mile distant city of Barville. There had been a shooting and the girl had been mixed up in it. So had Black Yankee. Convinced of the fact that she was a murderess — if unintentionally — the girl had packed her belongings and headed south — for Twin Pines, she had said. And now —

'Nice dame,' Black Yankee mused, and as he realized her attention had been caught by him he raised a hand and motioned. The girl hesitated in the haze, seeming to reflect, then she came slowly forward and reached the bar-counter.

'Still shooting your way around, Yankee, I see,' she commented, with a cynical curve of her lip.

'Yeah. Only way to stay healthy. Have a drink . . . '

'I'd rather not — with you.'

The outlaw's pale eyes fixed her. 'I don't like that kind of talk from a dame. Drink — and be sociable. Barkeep — give the lady what she wants.'

'I'll stick to lemonade,' she said briefly, and then relaxed against the bar, considering the outlaw dispassionately. 'You know,' she said, 'you're not fooling me a bit, Yankee. You've shot your way into this town — I saw you do it tonight — but it's not just for safety for yourself and these cut-throats who go around with you. It's to keep your paws on me, isn't it?'

'How'd you guess?' Black Yankee asked, grinning. 'Something else y'might as well remember too, kid. I know what happened when that guy Rolf Peterson got bumped off. I've only got to open my mouth wide enough to make the authorities mighty interested in you — and your whereabouts.'

'You wouldn't dare tell the authorities anything, Yankee. Not when you're on the run from them yourself.'

'You don't think I'd be fool enough to give 'em the tip-off that *I'm* givin' the information, do you? I ain't *that* loco. Jus' the same I'd get the news to 'em, if I'm so minded. Seems like you'd better be nice t'me, doesn't it? Just in case . . .'

'I didn't murder that man,' the girl stated deliberately. 'Somebody shot him dead and I happened to be there at the time. I picked up the gun and — Well, I guess I lost my head and ran for it.'

'Which'll make it look mighty bad to the police,' Black Yankee pointed out. 'Yuh ran straight into *me* when y'came out of Peterson's office. I could have put you in the clear but instead you was determined to make a break for it and come to Twin Pines here. Okay — so you came. An' I came after you. An' here we both are — happy and bright.'

'Which means you mean to hold it over me that I murdered Peterson.'

16

'Right,' the outlaw agreed, with brutal frankness. 'You can't prove otherwise, and I'm the only one who saw you leave that office. If your fingerprints get checked with those on the gun which wus found beside Peterson you'll be in a tough spot. But if yore sociable there ain't no reason why you should ever need to worry . . . And don't try blowin' town, neither. I'll find you wherever you go.'

Claire Henderson picked up the glass of lemonade the barkeep put down at her elbow and contemplated it thoughtfully. Without looking up, she said,

'Whilst you're being so smart, Yankee, doesn't it occur to you that I might tip-off the authorities where *you* are? They'd certainly like to know.'

The outlaw shrugged his broad shoulders. 'Tell 'em if you like. They'll get shot down as fast as they come after me. I've nothin' to lose if I kill the whole bunch of 'em. By accident it might so happen that you'd be shot too

17

— and that'd be just too bad, wouldn't it?'

'Yes . . . ' The girl looked deeply into the amber fluid with its gently stirring bubbles. 'Yes, wouldn't it?'

Black Yankee gave his deep-throated chuckle, took the girl's arm tightly and pressed it with his powerful fingers.

'There just ain't no need fur us to go on like this, kid. You an' me can do each other quite a lot of good if we stick together. Don't start makin' things tough for yourself. You've only got to be friendly, go on bein' hostess here, and leave it at that . . . In case you don't know, Steve Bradshaw ain't runnin' this joint any more. I'm doin' it.'

'Same as the rest of the town?' Claire Henderson asked. 'You're aiming to be sheriff, saloon owner, and maybe mayor — all in one?'

'Not mayor — he's too useful for keeping law an' order.' Black Yankee grinned and pushed his glass forward for it to be refilled. 'But I'll take care I run everything else . . . *my* way. Better be sensible about this business, kid.'

Claire Henderson did not answer. She drank her lemonade, put down the empty glass and then stood thinking. The outlaw made no comment. He stood watching her, his elbows propped on the counter. His pale, soulless eyes took in the details of her still young and slender figure, the straightness of her features, the fairness of her carefully coiffured hair. In any state she would have been considered above-average in looks.

'As long as you keep your distance, Yankee, I'll keep mine,' she said at last, with a direct look of her blue-grey eyes. 'Let it go at that.'

'Sure thing,' the outlaw agreed, with a readiness that seemed to suggest he had other plans in mind. 'In the meantime where are you stayin'? Might as well know where my hostess spends her off time.'

'I'm at the Wide Acres Hotel down the street — and I don't welcome visitors.'

Black Yankee grinned again. 'I won't be a visitor anyways. 'Bout time you started realizin' that I'm your new employer. Be nice to me, an' I reckon you'll find it well worth your while!'

2

Within two weeks Black Yankee's ruthless methods had made him — as he had intended from the first — the absolute ruler of Twin Pines. With his five cohorts, every one of them deadly accurate trigger-men, he brought to heel those few who looked like showing opposition — and in certain cases the low-hanging branches of the trees just outside the town bore a swinging corpse as a lesson to those who might have ideas about the future. Black Yankee was nothing if not thorough.

What exactly his plans were nobody seemed to know — and he did not say. Apparently he was content to live on the resources of Twin Pines, his guns being the one means of him getting what he wanted. He was more or less safe from the law, he believed, shut away in this little town of which he was the absolute dictator. How long this state of affairs might have continued nobody could guess, had not Thorn Tanworth ridden into town one evening.

He arrived at sunset — a hawklike, dusty man with broad shoulders and taut muscles, dressed entirely in black with the dirt of the trail smothering his sweat-stained shirt. He came into the main street from the Catalina trail as though he were a part of his mare, so easily did he ride. It was a loping step at which he urged his mount, his agate-blue eyes glancing from side to side of him as he moved. Then a cowpuncher on the boardwalk suddenly recognized him in the twilight and came running across the dusty street towards him.

'Thorn! Darn me if it ain't Thorn Tanworth! Ain't seen you in five years. Where've you bin puttin' yuhself?'

Thorn Tanworth, son of the dead Sheriff Tanworth, was perhaps thirty years old. In the five years he had been away from Twin Pines he seemed to have aged twenty. He was thin-featured, taut-mouthed, with an unfriendly stare in his eyes.

'I suppose I should know you?' he asked, halting his mare and looking down on the puncher.

'Know me? Blast it, didn't we rope steers together when you was here? — afore your dad packed you off t' make a man of yuh?'

Thorn Tanworth's mouth twisted for a moment into a hard smile.

'Yeah — I remember. Shorty Alroyd . . . That's you, isn't it?' Then before the puncher could answer he continued, 'I heard that my dad had been wiped out. Suits me fine: I c'n come back into town with the old buzzard out of the way. The guy who rubbed out my old man did me a mighty big favour.'

Shorty Alroyd looked uncertain, frowning, and scratching his grizzled cheek.

'Look, feller, yore sorta different,' he said uneasily. 'I don't reckon to know how deep the difference wus between you an' your old man, but it seems kinda hard to believe that you're *that* glad to be rid of him.'

The hard-faced young man was silent for a moment, his agate-blue eyes looking down the street, then he asked:

'Know how much the memory of the old man means to me?'

The puncher shook his head; then he started as Thorn Tanworth spat viciously into the dust.

'That much,' he said coldly, pushing his Stetson up on his forehead. 'Since that's made clear let's have no more worries over the old devil. He killed my mom, you know — years afore her time. Browbeat the daylights outa her. Reckon I never forgave him for that . . . Gettin' back to cases, who took care of the old boy?'

'Black Yankee and his dirty outlaws. Can't rightly say which of 'em since they all fired at once.' Shorty Alroyd gave a grim look. 'He — Black Yankee I mean — shot Steve Bradshaw too, but that wus self-defence. You're in an outlaw town now, feller. Black Yankee's seed to that.'

The young, mahogany-faced man was silent, musing. Then he asked: 'Where'd I find this killer?'

'Right now I guess he'll be in the Lucky Horseshoe. He seems to have taken it over amongst other things.'

'Thanks.'

Thorn Tanworth spurred his mare gently and went up the street, sliding from the saddle when he had reached the saloon. Its windows were already lighted with the glow of the oil lamps behind them and the noise of the drink den came floating out into the soft, cool air of the evening. Thorn patted his twin .45s, tied the mare's reins to the tie-rack, then strode up the steps and through the batwings. Beyond them he paused for a moment, thumbs latched on to his pants belt, his agate-blue eyes studying the smoky scene. His eyes strayed beyond the fair-haired Claire Henderson in the distance, as she went about her usual task of hostess, to the big, broad-shouldered man standing near the bar keeping an eye on the 'customers'.

With long, easy strides Thorn Tanworth moved to the bar counter and ordered a brandy. The barkeep gave a start when he noticed him.

'Thorn! Say, feller, I — '

'Shut up and give me the brandy,' Thorn answered curtly.

'Eh? What kind of greetin' is that fur a pal? You an' me usta get on mighty well together, Thorn, afore you left town and yet now — '

'Blast you, where's that drink?' Thorn demanded. 'Button your lip and hurry!'

His tone was so loud it was impossible for Black Yankee, at the further end of the bar, not to hear it. Chewing a cheroot he came forward and considered Thorn curiously. To Black Yankee it was a surprise to find a man slightly bigger than himself. This nut-brown young man with the power-packed arms and shoulders was all of six feet four.

'Stranger 'round here?' the outlaw enquired. 'You sound like a guy who's usta gettin' things done.'

Thorn looked at Black Yankee dispassionately. 'Yeah — sure I am. Only common sense, isn't it?'

'S'pose so. Anyways, it's what I like . . . Stranger around here?'

'Course he ain't,' the barkeep growled, planking down the brandy. 'He was born in this town, and lived in it until his old man threw him out. Leastways, that wus what it looked like.'

'Old man?' the outlaw repeated. 'Who?'

'I'm the son of Sheriff Tanworth,' Thorn answered calmly, and drained his brandy at a gulp, adding, 'Another — and make it quick.'

Black Yankee's expression changed somewhat. His eyes strayed to the young giant's guns, then back to his grim brown face.

'Son of the sheriff, huh? We had reason to rub him out — an' if you've come to start gettin' a bead on me 'cos of it you're on mighty dangerous ground, feller.'

'If I'd come for that reason I could have blown the heart out of you the moment I entered the doors,' Thorn answered. 'I didn't — an' I won't. Chiefly because I think you an' me speak the same language.'

'Yeah?' Black Yankee looked suspicious. 'I don't get it. We eliminate your old man and you want to be friends because of it. Sump'n queer some place. I've lived long enough t'know that blood's thicker'n water.'

Thorn swallowed his second brandy and then looked about him.

'You've taken over this place, I hear — so I s'pose you've taken the office over too? What say we go there and drink and talk in peace? I think you an' me might do things together.'

'Okay,' Black Yankee shrugged. 'This way — '

He led Thorn round the end of the bar and to a door at the back. Pushing it open he motioned into an office and Thorn went in ahead of him, sitting on a chair next to the desk. Black Yankee took the swivel chair and crossed his legs, swinging himself gently to and fro. There was suspicion still in his pale eyes as Thorn considered him steadily, remarking to himself that this outlaw was quite one of the ugliest men he had ever seen — save for the richness of his oily black hair.

'Well, what's the set-up?' Black Yankee asked. 'I haven't all night to waste.'

'It goes without sayin',' Thorn said, rolling himself a cigarette deftly, 'that you're a wanted man. The authorities in nearly every state are on the prod for you.'

'So what?' Black Yankee asked menacingly. 'That's one reason why I took over this town and buried myself and my boys. And if yore thinkin' of giving infurmation about — '

'I'm not. I'm on the run myself.'

'You are?' The outlaw gave a start.

'Well — say now, that sort of makes sense.'

'I thought it would. Mebbe I'd better go back a bit . . . ' Thorn lighted his cigarette and then continued. 'Five years ago my old man — and he had mighty holy ideas that made my scalp crawl — figgered I was wastin' away my time in this town, so he booted me out and told me to make my own way. I s'pose he thought I'd go to a city and fix myself up in a nice quiet job or sump'n — but I've too much of the outdoors in me for that. I took to robbin' freight trains instead. I got away with it for a while, then somethin' went wrong and I had to lie low for a time. It so happened that I got my hands on a printing set — *how* is my business — so I thought I might do worse than try printing a few of Uncle Sam's bills . . . Like this.'

Thorn took a wad of dollar bills from his pocket and threw them on the desk. He motioned with a long, sinewy hand.

'Take a look,' he invited. 'If y'can see

what's wrong with 'em yore the only man who can.'

Frowning to himself, interested and yet determined not to show it, Black Yankee stripped three of the bills from under the rubber band and studied them carefully. He turned them over and over, held them to the light, snapped them between his fingers, and finally tossed them down.

'I've got to admit it,' he sighed. 'They'd fool me any place. An' if they'd fool me they'd fool anybody.'

'Right,' Thorn agreed. 'If that ain't a basis for a partnership, I don't know what is.'

'Partnership? Meaning what?'

'Technically,' Thorn said, 'you're lying low here to keep out of the way of the authorities. I heard that much on my travels, which was one reason why I decided to come here too. You've turned this into an outlaws' town, where any guy or gal on the run can have sanctuary. I'm claimin' that right as a fellow fugitive — but with somethin' more. I can forge all the dollar bills you'll ever need, and I will if you'll give me a fifty-fifty share in runnin' this town.'

Black Yankee shook his head. 'No dice, feller. You oughta know that there can't be two bosses for one setup. I don't need your unlimited dollar supply so badly that I'm willin' to share runnin' this town with you.'

'I can of course be on my way,' Thorn reflected. 'And whilst I *am* on my way I can so fix it that the authorities get to know yore hiding here — And bang will go your quiet little tin-horn dictator-ship.'

The two men sat measuring each other for a moment, then Thorn shrugged his massive shoulders.

'Only I don't want it that way. Too dangerous for me, and ruins everythin' for you. When we're both outside the law that ain't the right way to act ... We should work together, and between us we can not only run this town but plenty of others in time ... Don't get me wrong, Yankee. I don't want to give orders, boss the folks around, and stand watchin' things with my thumbs hooked in my belt. I'll be that darned busy with a printing press in a quiet corner I'll leave all the bossin' around to you. Only I *do* demand a say in most things that are planned.'

'What things?' Black Yankee asked, thinking.

'You're sittin' in the middle of rich ranchland, feller.' Thorn gave a grim smile. 'I was born here, remember, and I know just how much cattle wealth there is within a hundred miles. You don't suppose thousands of steers are goin' to be left untouched while we just sit on our backsides, do you?'

'Y'mean, rustlin'?'

'Exactly — rustling. I've got contacts in this region — the sort of contacts you can only make if you've lived here since bein' a nipper. Better think it over, Yankee. Between us we can do nicely for ourselves. Since we're both more or less in each other's hands I can't see what there is against you agreein' teamin' up with me.'

'Well . . . all right,' Black Yankee said finally, studying his cheroot. 'But I'm warnin' you. See that you stay clear of anythin' that's my personal interest — or property.'

'F'rinstance?'

'The Lucky Horseshoe for one thing. I'll run it as I see fit, including the gaming tables.'

'If you want to play crooked gambling that's your affair,' Thorn shrugged.

'Who said anythin' about being crooked?' Yankee snapped.

'Nobody. Sort of goes without saying.'

Again the eyes of the men met, steadily, the inner distrust of each man for the other only slightly masked.

'There's somethin' else,' the outlaw added. 'There's a gal in the saloon by the name of Claire Henderson — '

'I saw her. Good looker . . . '

'Just keep your mitts off her, Tanworth, that's all. She belongs to me.'

Thorn gave his hard smile. 'Yeah? She know about it?'

Black Yankee clenched his fist for a moment and then relaxed as he saw Thorn's body tauten slightly in anticipation of trouble.

'Yeah, she knows about it,' Yankee said. 'And I'm warnin' *you*.'

'Okay — I shan't take her away from you if that's what you're 'fraid of, but if I decide to talk to her — just for the pleasure of exchangin' words with a nice gal — I'll do it. And you won't be able to stop me.'

'Just as long as it gets no further,' Yankee said.

Thorn considered his cigarette for a moment, then:

'That's settled then. We work together. I'll put up at the roomin' house down the street — Ma Brendick's. She knows me well enough. Tomorrow we'll straighten things out a bit — decidin' what we do an' how we do it. My main concern from now on is to get my hands on printin' apparatus, and that seems to tell me that I'll have to take over the runnin' of the *Twin Pines News*.'

Yankee rubbed his jaw pensively. 'Okay — but I don't quite see how takin' over the local paper is goin' to help you make dollar bills.'

'I don't want the paper,' Thorn grinned. 'Old Benson can keep it — do what he likes with it. All I want is control of his printing equipment. I've got the plates for my dollar bill stuff with me in my saddle-bag. I need a press, special inks, and stuff you can only get if you're in the printin' line. I'll see old Benson and fix him so he doesn't guess what I'm aimin' at. He knows me well enough.'

'And supposin' he opens his mouth too wide? I reckon it'd be safer if he was taken care of and you take over the paper.'

Thorn shook his head. 'Wouldn't do.

Y'can go just so far with these people, Yankee — an' no further. Shootin' old Benson might set fire to the tinder and you and your boys, and me included, 'd be in a hot spot . . . No, leave Benson to me. I'll convince him everything's on the up-an'-up. He's always thought of me as a good little lad.'

'Have it your own way — but it's always seemed to me that a dead man is much safer than a live one.'

Thorn got to his feet. 'Seems to be all for now,' he said, dropping his cigarette and then crushing his heel down on to it. 'We'll do some more talkin' tomorrow. If you want me in the meantime you know where Ma Brendick's is.'

With a casual nod he left the office and returned to the smoke-hazy expanse of the saloon. It was pure chance which caused him to nearly collide with Claire Henderson as she came round the bar. Thorn caught her arm and steadied her, then pushed his hat further back on his forehead and surveyed her insolently.

'Well,' he murmured. 'I didn't know they had gals as good-lookin' as you around Twin Pines.'

The girl's grey-blue eyes studied him. She gave a little shrug.

'All right, so I'm good-looking,' she said. 'How far does that get us?'

'No tellin'. Depends how far you want to go.'

'I've gone quite far enough, and so have you. Now if you'll excuse me I've my job to get on with as hostess and — '

The girl paused and looked beyond Thorn. He turned to see Black Yankee standing with his back to the door of the office, grim menace on his ugly face.

'Not wastin' much time, Tanworth, are yuh?' he asked briefly.

'We collided,' Thorn explained, shrugging.

'Yeah? S'posin' I don't choose to believe that?'

'It happens to be right,' Claire snapped. 'And anyways, what on earth's the matter with both you men? You don't think I give a darn what you think about *me*, do you?'

'I reckon you've a reason for liking *me*, anyway,' Black Yankee said.

The girl did not answer but a look of loathing, not unmixed with fear, crossed her pretty face for a moment. Thorn noticed it but his expression did not give anything away. He said briefly:

'I said that if I wanted to talk to the gal I'd do it, Yankee. An' you can't stop me!'

'I may — if I'm so minded.'

There was a grim pause, Thorn with his fists clenched and Black Yankee with one powerful hand dropped to the butt of his right-side gun. Then the girl turned and swung away without another word.

'Pity she ain't more sociable,' Thorn sighed, looking after her. 'Not that I can blame her if she thinks all the guys in this town are more or less like you, Yankee . . . Anyways, be seein' you in the mornin'.'

3

The following morning Thorn Tanworth visited old Josiah Benson, the owner and publisher of the *Twin Pines News*. With one boy of about fourteen he handled all the news that ever came into the town — and he handled it fearlessly. Or at least such had been the case until Black Yankee had ridden into town. Now the white-haired man, who believed that truth should come before everything, found himself in the position of having to print lies, if only to save himself from receiving a bullet through his heart. He had to say nice things about Black Yankee — or take the consequences.

His troubles were magnified enormously when, looking up from the galley proofs of the latest edition, he found himself gazing down the barrel of a levelled .45. His eyes rose to the young mahogany face under the big Stetson.

'Thorn!' he ejaculated. 'Thorn Tanworth! I'll be dad-blamed. What brought you back into town, youngster?'

'Plenty of things, Benson — an' I'm not the youngster I was. I've bin around, see?'

The old man smiled. 'You always were a kid for jokin'. Put the hardware away. Yore makin' me nervous.'

'I know; that's what I want to do. You an' me have some talkin' to do, an' I want to convince you I'm right.'

Josiah Benson's expression slowly changed. He sank down on a chair beside the big hand-printing press.

'What's the idea?' he asked bluntly. 'From the way you're behavin' I could almost think you're Black Yankee. I always figgered we were friends. Known you since you was a boy an' — '

'Cut out the mush,' Thorn said curtly. 'I'm here on business. Each day after you've finished with your presses

41

— which I remember is around six o'clock — I want the use of 'em.'

'What for?'

'That's my business.' Thorn grinned cynically. 'Mebbe I'm going to print a book on my experiences since my old man threw me outa town. Anyway, that's what I want — and what's more it's what I mean to *have*.'

Josiah Benson was silent, rubbing the back of his neck in bewilderment. Thorn's agate-blue eyes strayed to the watching, listening youngster at the far end of the room.

'Blow, you!' Thorn snapped, glaring at him. 'An' don't ever come back or I'll skin the hide off you.' Then after the boy had scuttled and the glass-fronted door had slammed Thorn looked back impatiently at Benson. 'Well, dad, come on! What's it to be?'

'Don't leave me much choice, d'you, with that rod pokin' at me?' Benson asked agrievedly. 'I'd say 'yes' gladly if you'd come an' asked me in a civilized way — 'stead of like a blamed outlaw.'

'I *am* an outlaw — same as Black Yankee — and that mebbe is what causes it. All right — where's the key to the joint? When you finish for the day I want to be able to get in here without havin' t' break the door down.'

Deliberately Benson fumbled for a key ring in his pants pocket, stripped one of the keys from it, and handed it over. The bewildered look was still in his eyes.

'I may be later than usual finishing,' he said. 'Now you've sent that lad away. He was the only help I had.'

'You don't need him. Kids at his age are curious — *too* curious for my likin'. I'm taking no chances. What I'm figgerin' doing with your printing equipment isn't exactly . . . legal.'

'Which means I might get into a spot, too!'

'Not if you keep your nose clean. All you've got to do is just as you've always done; an' I'll take care of myself. I won't break anything; I won't mess anythin' up. I'll just use your stuff.'

43

Benson, the first shock of events seeming to have subsided somewhat, got slowly to his feet. For several moments he stood regarding the bronzed young man fixedly.

'Look, Thorn,' he said finally. 'Why don't you give it to me neat? What's all this about? The last thing I can imagine about you is that you're an outlaw — though I s'pose it's possible in the five years you've been away. An' I find it even tougher to figger out what you're aimin' to do in this town.'

'I'm aiming to run it,' Thorn said deliberately, and put his gun back in its holster.

'*Run* it! Black Yankee does that already — or didn't you know?'

'Sure I know. Him an' me have already had words on that. For the moment we're going to run it between us. But,' Thorn added pensively, 'for your edification I don't mind tellin' you that I think I've a more legitimate right to run Twin Pines than Black Yankee has. I was born here, which makes a difference. Later, mebbe, I'll take care of that angle. Right now I'm in on all deals he makes, as well as runnin' a private scheme on my own for which I need your presses.'

'You can only need presses and printing equipment for two things, lad — printing or counterfeiting. If you've any sense it ain't counterfeiting.'

'S'pose you let *me* do the worryin', huh? I'm an outlaw anyway. Doesn't matter much what I do, be it on the side of th' law or against it.' Thorn straightened his hat and nodded. 'That's all for now, I reckon. I'll take over this evenin'.'

He turned and went out, leaving Benson staring after him with mystification in his eyes. Grim-faced, Thorn reached the boardwalk and stood thinking for a moment, considering the busy street with the men and women and buckboards and teams going back and forth — then he turned and strode along the boardwalk to the Lucky Horseshoe.

Inside he found it dim and fetid with the previous night's tobacco fumes. The barkeep and a couple of waiters were busy with mops and buckets. The chairs were piled up in wooden porcupines on top of the stripped tables.

'Yankee around?' Thorn asked the barkeep, and the man nodded as he drew the back of his hand over his streaming face.

'In his office — only he's engaged. Miss Henderson's with him.'

'Don't worry me none,' Thorn said, and striding over to the office door he thumped on it once and then strode in. He was just in time to see Black Yankee drop his hands from the girl's shoulders as she drew back from him sharply.

'Mornin',' Thorn said, cuffing his hat on to his forehead.

Claire Henderson looked at him coldly and Black Yankee gave a glare.

'What the hell's the idea of bustin' in here when I'm busy?'

'Busy doin' what?' Thorn's eyes strayed to the girl and he jerked his head to her significantly. 'Better get outa here, kid, before Yankee gets overheated,' he said.

The outlaw swallowed something and went a shade darker under his tan.

'You blasted no-account!' he exploded. 'What in blazes has it got to do with you what — '

'I'm going anyway,' Claire Henderson snapped. 'And next time, Yankee, when you want to tell me what my duties are in the evening don't be so demonstrative!'

She left the office and the door slammed. Thorn raised his eyebrows and then lounged indolently with his elbows on top of the roll desk.

'I saw Benson,' he said.

'Damn Benson! Look, Tanworth, if you bust in here again an' interrupt me when I'm talkin' to Claire Henderson I'll — '

'Claire Henderson, huh? So that's the gal's name? I rather like it.'

'Then you'll better start *unliking* it, quick. Remember what I told you about

47

her. She belongs to me — '

'Okay, okay, keep your shirt on,' Thorn murmured easily. 'Just don't start maulin' her around too much, that's all. I don't like to see it . . . Now, gettin' back to cases. I've seen Benson and fixed it so's I can use his printing equipment. I figger he doesn't quite like the idea, but he'll have to put up with it. So, that squares that off.'

'All right,' Yankee growled uncivilly. 'That's your worry anyways — nothin' to do with me.'

Thorn reflected for a moment and then sat down at the desk and plonked his hat on it. He smoothed the untidy dark hair back from his forehead.

'It's time we made our plans, Yankee. As I told you last night, there's cattle for the pickin' up around here. How soon can you go into action?'

'Rustlin', you mean? Any time you like; but first I've got to know how you fit into the setup.'

'That's an easy one. I'll draw a plan of where the best ranches are and you'll provide the boys — and control 'em — for the job. I don't have to tell you that they'd better be hand-picked ones. If you use any of the locals they'll do all they can to turn informers, and that'll finish us . . . At the northern end of this valley there's a narrow ravine. We can drive the cattle through that. Have to work it out in detail. I can also arrange buyers for the steers who'll change the brands. With the money we get paid — and we'll see it's in dollar bills and no cheques — we'll add a similar amount of forged money. With the good and bad money mixed up, we've a better chance of gettin' away with it. Right?'

'Yeah — sounds okay. And I s'pose you want to cut fifty-fifty on whatever we get for the cattle?'

'What do you think? And there's another thing,' Thorn added, his piercing eyes fixed on the outlaw's face. 'Don't get any bright notions, Yankee. Once you have the plans in your hands I reckon there isn't anythin' to stop you tryin' to blot me out. I've thought of that. I trust you as much as I would a snake. To guard against it I've got a counter-plan fixed — and it'll knock you right out if you try anythin' on me. Savvy?'

Yankee glared, but did not say anything. With a grim smile Thorn got to his feet.

'All right, we'll leave it at that. I'll drop along to the Lucky Horseshoe this evening with the plan all doped out. See you then . . . '

* * *

It was after sunset when Thorn appeared in the Lucky Horseshoe. During the day nobody seemed to have seen him about the town. Presumably he had been busy in Ma Brendick's rooming house working out his plans for a rustling raid. Black Yankee, standing at the bar, was far too busy paying attention to Claire Henderson to notice that Thorn had arrived.

50

'Any more manhandling from you, Yankee, and I'll tell the authorities where you are and take the consequences,' the girl breathed angrily, her eyes glinting. 'It's getting so that you can't keep your filthy paws off me — '

'That any way to be sociable?' Yankee grinned. 'All I ask is that you have a drink with me — as any hostess should, seein' as I'm your employer an' the owner of this joint — and mebbe hand out a kiss for luck. What's wrong with that?'

'Plenty,' Thorn said, and leaned one elbow on the bar counter.

The girl and Black Yankee swung round to look at him. Deep, malevolent fury glowed suddenly in the outlaw's face.

'You makin' this a habit?' he demanded.

'Could be,' Thorn shrugged, and to the barkeep he added: 'Small brandy.'

Claire Henderson looked from one man to the other, her hands on her hips, her jaw set.

'To my mind,' she said coldly, 'there's nothing much to choose between either of you beasts. The only difference is that you, Yankee, can't keep your hands off me — whilst you — whatever your name is — are only supposed to be protecting me so you can do the same thing.'

Thorn took up his glass of brandy. 'Thorn Tanworth's the name, Miss Henderson. Son of the former sheriff.'

'And he ran you out of town,' the girl said scornfully. 'I've heard all about that. I suspected you were his son, but I wasn't sure. Now I *am* sure I'm less interested than ever . . . '

She turned away angrily and wandered between the tables, amidst the haze of tobacco fumes. Thorn watched her go and played with his brandy glass. Yankee stood watching him, his ugly face still contorted with a murderous scowl.

'I've been thinkin' . . . ' Thorn said presently, musing. 'These plans I've laid are too complicated for there to be two bosses to run 'em, Yankee. Like you said — can't be two big boys at the top.'

'Glad you found it out,' Yankee sneered. 'Sooner you blow town and take your blasted forging contraptions with you the better.'

'You've gotten the idea wrong, feller; I'm not blowin' any place. It's you that's goin' — chiefly becos I don't like the way you treat Claire Henderson. She ain't my type, mind — but she's a woman, an' I don't like to see 'em knocked around by an ornery cuss like you.'

Black Yankee's lips quivered slightly with passion.

'Don't know whether you remember it or not,' Thorn went on in his easy voice, 'but way back in the old days, when outlaw towns sprang up overnight, they ran 'em on jungle law. If one guy figgered he was better'n the top man he challenged him to prove his authority. If he won — *he* became top man. If he lost, he went out feet first. Remember?'

'Sure I remember. You gettin' the crazy idea that you c'n run this town better 'n me?'

'Yeah. Ain't crazy, either. For one thing, I'd treat the women straight; for another, I've bin thinkin' I'd be an all-time sucker to split my information with you, Yankee.'

The outlaw smiled crookedly. 'You talk mighty tough, Tanworth, but I don't see you doin' much.'

'Yeah, right enough,' agreed a scrub-jawed puncher at a nearby table. 'Words is cheap around here, feller.'

Thorn played with his brandy glass and looked at the puncher levelly.

'Sidin' with Black Yankee, huh?' he asked. 'Got the quaint idea that I don't mean what I say?'

'Words,' the puncher said derisively. 'Nothin' but words! We all know you was run out of town because you couldn't stand up for yourself, an' the thought was too much fer your old man. You ain't changed, I reckon, in spite of your fancy hardware.' Abruptly, with such terrific speed nobody could follow the movement, Thorn's right hand blurred down to his holster. He whipped out his gun, levelled, and fired all in one movement. The puncher at the table stared dazedly for a moment, his hand clamping to his right breast and coming away stained in red. With a low, choking gasp he collapsed on the floor.

'If it's action you want, you got it,' Thorn explained, looking about him with steely eyes. 'I don't allow no guy to talk to me like that — You!' he snapped to the remaining puncher at the table. 'Get that guy outa town. Take him as far as the mesa and dump him. It's the safest place . . . An' don't get any bright ideas on the way. Only one law in this town — and that's mine.'

Black Yankee stared fixedly, too astonished to say anything for the moment. Amidst a grim hush, whilst the rest of the saloon's habitués looked on — Claire Henderson amongst them — the cowpuncher lifted the fallen man from the floor. He felt at the red-stained chest for a moment, and then looked up grimly.

'You shoot straight, anyways,' he muttered. 'The guy's finished.'

'Best thing for him,' Thorn said, reholstering his gun. 'Get him out!'

The puncher obeyed, and every eye followed him as he carried the body out of the saloon. Shootings were not uncommon in the Lucky Horseshoe, but few were carried out with such ruthless deliberation. Then Black Yankee took a deep breath.

'All right, so you can shoot straight,' he said. 'That don't make no difference to me. I'm top man around here — not you.'

Thorn picked up his brandy glass and studied it — then in one movement he flung the stinging spirit clean into the outlaw's face. He staggered and gasped, clawing at his eyes. In those brief seconds his two guns were snatched from their holsters and a fist crashed with cataclysmic violence into his chin. Dazed, half-blinded with the brandy, he reeled against the bar counter and only just saved himself from falling.

'Might as well settle this issue right now,' Thorn explained, putting his own guns on the bar counter beside Yankee's. 'Since I've decided to take over, I'll have to prove I'm worth it — '

The anguish in his eyes abating, the outlaw straightened up, doubled his fist, and then threw himself on Thorn. Thorn side-stepped at the last second, whirled round a bunched left and landed it with smashing impact on the back of the outlaw's ox-like neck. He rocked and gulped, the pain jarring straight down his spine — but he did not collapse.

Immediately Thorn followed up his advantage with a left and a right in quick succession. He would have landed a terrific uppercut, but it missed its mark, and instead he took a punishing blow in the stomach. Winded, he gulped for a second, and half fell on one of the tables, only to collapse amidst it as Yankee hurled himself on him and bore him down.

Each holding the other in a steel grip, the two men rolled about the floor, striving for a single objective — the other's throat. Black Yankee succeeded first, his knotty fingers sinking deep into Thorn's windpipe. He thrashed, bent his legs, twisted, strained with every ounce of his power-packed arms and shoulders, but the clutch was relentless. As the struggle to breathe became more desperate he relaxed slightly — then with a sudden vast effort he slammed his knee upward and twisted sideways at the same time. The impact dislodged Yankee slightly, and a piston-rod blow clean in the face shook him completely free. In those few seconds he was under Thorn and receiving a hail of blows to the face and mouth.

How long Thorn might have maintained his onslaught was something none of the onlookers could guess.

Somehow Black Yankee forced himself sideways at a crucial moment, and what would have been a knockout blow hit the floor instead. Thorn gasped at the impact of his knuckles, then jerked upwards and backwards at a left-handed punch under the chin.

The small of his back brought up hard against the bar counter, and it saved him from falling. He saw Black Yankee, his unlovely face blood-streaked, hurtling towards him. He abruptly bent sideways and slammed round his right at the same instant. The force of the punch, landing under the right side of his jaw, knocked the outlaw clean off balance and he landed on his face on the floor. There he stopped, breathing hard, Thorn standing over him waiting for the next.

'Okay . . . ' Black Yankee whispered, screwing round his bruised face and looking up. 'Okay — you win.'

Thorn twisted his fingers in Yankee's collar and whirled him to his feet. Then he swung him round and propelled him towards the batwings.

'Hit the trail, Yankee, an' don't ever come back,' he said briefly, and with a final mighty shove he sent the outlaw stumbling out on to the boardwalk and then into the dust of the street.

With brisk strides Thorn returned to the bar counter, holstered his own guns and picked up the outlaw's. He took them out on the boardwalk and threw them down to him.

'You may need 'em,' he said curtly, ''specially out on the trail. Never bin my code to turn even a killer loose without the means to protect himself. Now get goin' — and stay goin'!'

Black Yankee said nothing. He picked up his guns and then slowly hauled himself to his feet. Thorn watched him for a moment and then came back into the saloon, feeling tenderly at the bruises about his face and body. When he reached the bar counter he stood looking about him.

Nobody spoke. Some were looking scared, others malevolent — and Claire

Henderson in the background was gazing in cold scorn.

'You!' Thorn said abruptly, motioning to the short, tubby mayor at the rear of the crowd. 'Come over here!'

The mayor obeyed and stood blinking and waiting uneasily. Thorn stooped and from the floor picked up the sheriff's badge which had been torn from Yankee's shirt in the struggle. He held it out.

'Swear me in,' he ordered. 'Twin Pine's got a new sheriff whether it likes it or not — an' as the son of one of its former sheriffs I'll do what I think is right for justice.'

'And for yourself,' Claire Henderson commented, folding her slender bare arms.

Thorn glanced at her but did not say anything. He repeated the words of the oath after the mayor and then waited whilst the badge was pinned on his shirt. The ceremony over he looked about him again.

'There's something you folks had

better start getting straight right now,' he said grimly. 'Black Yankee turned this into an outlaw town — a sanctuary for men and women who are on the run from the law, but he didn't make it clear what would happen if some of you didn't agree to the notion. So, now I've taken his place, I'll do it instead. If any man or woman here breathes one word to the authorities as to what this town's become — or that I'm here in hidin' — I'll shoot to kill. And don't think I couldn't do it. You saw what happened to that puncher just now. I'd do the same to anybody else if necessary.'

Nobody spoke. Thorn smiled tautly and added,

'I know most of you are against me — hence the warning; but at least five of you are with me, I reckon. You boys who were behind Black Yankee until I threw him out.'

The five trigger-men in the forefront who had ridden into town with the outlaw in the first instance glanced at each other and then turned back to Thorn and nodded.

'I reckon that's right enough,' assented the one called Jeff. 'We don't particklarly mind who we're workin' fur, so long as he's on the run as we are.'

'Good,' Thorn nodded. 'Then it's up to you boys to see that none of the folks in here try any funny business in attemptin' to get the authorities here. Since we've an outlaw town we're goin' to behave as outlaws. I want to know how many of you are behind me in cleanin' up some of the cattle from the neighbouring ranches.'

The hands of the five punchers rose immediately, then — half-heartedly — the hands of another half dozen rose too.

'Okay,' Thorn said, looking about him. 'Now to something else. Since I'm running this outfit from now on I want to find out which one of you is the best trigger-man of the lot.'

'I am,' Jeff said curtly. 'Only one man

could be quicker, I reckon — Yankee himself.'

'Words are cheap,' Thorn commented with a cynical smile. 'As that puncher told me . . . ' He looked around him and finally his gaze settled on the nearest kerosene lamp, depending from its thin steel wire out of the ceiling.

'Shoot that wire through in a straight pull from your holster an' I'll believe you,' he said. 'Go to it — And watch out below you mugs.'

There was a sudden scattering of the people from beneath the lamp. Jeff waited until they had moved aside then he whipped out his right-hand .44 and fired. With an abrupt twang the wire parted and the lamp crashed, stamped on immediately to smother the flames which spurted from the spilled oil. Thorn stood looking at the remaining piece of wire hanging from the roof.

'Nice goin',' he commented. 'Okay, Jeff, you're my right-hand man from now on. Tomorrow we go into a huddle to decide how best to get those cattle from nearby ranches . . . '

'Somethin' I'd like to know,' Jeff said, an air of menace about him as he returned his gun to its holster. 'How much do we get out of it? Us boys, I mean?'

'You get your cut,' Thorn told him calmly. 'Money paid for work done.'

'I reckon it should be fifty-fifty,' Jeff said. 'Fifty per. fer you an' fifty per. split between the five of us.'

'Then you're crazy. You'll get your cut, an' like it. Why d'you think I got rid of Black Yankee? If he'd have stayed boss and we'd have split fifty-fifty on our deals you mugs wouldn't even have had beer money. An' Jeff, since you'll be my right hand man, where do I find you if I want you in a hurry?'

'Room 7 — Ma Brendick's,' Jeff growled. 'We're all stayin' there . . . '

'Okay. Tomorrow we'll talk things over.'

4

Thorn, postponing for the time being his intention to use Josiah Benson's printing equipment, did not leave the Lucky Horseshoe until its usual closing time towards midnight. Since he had taken over the saloon instead of Black Yankee he was automatically its boss. Throughout the evening he sat at a corner table, drinking little and watching everything. Now and again he seemed to be figuring things out on a sheet of paper.

Once or twice he caught sight of Claire Henderson, but she did not come over to him. Evidently she had decided that one boss was as good as another. At closing time, however, as Thorn was taking a last look round before leaving and shutting up the place, he saw her waiting for him beside the batwings. Languidly, he strolled over to her, cigarette drooping from the corner of his mouth.

'Wantin' an escort?' he asked her briefly, and she tightened her belt about her coat with a certain meaning emphasis.

'Wouldn't be much sense in choosing a killer for that job, would there?' she asked coldly.

'Have it your own way — just askin'.' Thorn motioned out on to the board-walk and locked the saloon doors.

Then he turned to her again. 'What *do* you want, then, if it isn't my company?'

'Am I to assume,' the girl asked, 'that you've become my new employer?'

'Yeah. I know it gets confusin'. First it was Steve Bradshaw, then Black Yankee — now me. Any objections?'

'Plenty. I'm leaving tomorrow morning for Bluff Point. I want it to be a legal departure so I'm giving you notice, as my employer, and it's in operation right now. Good night!'

The girl began striding away then.

Thorn's lazy voice made her pause.

'Seems kinda funny to me that you walk out on me yet you didn't on Black Yankee. Mebbe we're both killers — but he's a darned sight blacker-hearted than I ever was. How come you stayed with him and won't stay with me? Or don't that rate an answer?'

Thorn came up to the girl as he spoke. In the wavering lights from the street kerosene lamps her expression was grim.

'I had my reasons for sticking beside Black Yankee,' she said.

'Couldn't be for love — the way he mauled you around. Only one other reason — He must have had a hold over you.'

'Supposing he had?' the girl demanded. 'Nothing to do with you, is it?'

'Nope, I reckon not — 'cept for one thing. Black Yankee isn't dead, you know. He may be anywheres around these parts, but too yellow to come back into town. If he spots you leavin' anything might happen.'

'I'll risk it,' the girl retorted, and went on her way.

Thorn watched her go, rolling himself a cigarette in the gloom. He lighted it and lounged against the tie rail for a while, making no attempt to go on to Ma Brendick's rooming house. Finally, when perhaps twenty minutes had passed, he turned about and went back to the Lucky Horseshoe, letting himself into the fumy, heavy atmosphere and locking the door behind him.

He went over to one of the tables, lit a small oil lamp and, holding it before him to see his way, he went across to the wooden panel wall nearest the bar. Carefully, the light of the lamp moving in a slow deliberate circle, he inspected the woodwork. Finally, dissatisfied, he hauled up a table, stood on it, and inspected the panelling from a higher angle.

'Mmmm!' he murmured at length, and tugged his jack-knife from his pocket. With great care he finally

69

extracted a .44 bullet — the one which Lefty had fired when he had split the lamp wire — and tossed it up and down in his palm.

'Mebbe right — mebbe wrong,' he muttered. 'Worth a try. I — '

He stopped and turned sharply at a sudden sound in the gloom. It was a click, followed by the faint squeak of a hinge. Immediately he whirled his lamp round and its light fell upon Claire Henderson as she stood shielding her eyes from the glare.

'What in hell do you want here?' Thorn demanded angrily, jumping down from the table and striding over to her. 'What right have you to — '

'Oh, so it's you,' she interrupted, as he lowered the beam. 'Technically, you know, I could ask the same question. Not exactly normal to find you standing on a table with a lamp in your hand inspecting the wall . . . '

'I said what are *you* doing here?'

'I've come for my evening dress. I forgot when I gave my notice that I'd left it behind in the dressing room. Can't afford to lose it; cost me quite a few dollars.'

'So that's it — How'd you get in? I locked the door!'

'Why?' Claire Henderson asked.

'Never mind why,' Thorn breathed. 'How *did* you get in?'

The girl fished in her pocket and finally held up a key. She put it in Thorn's hand.

'Steve Bradshaw was an honest man,' she said quietly. 'He knew that my proper status as hostess here was as second-in-charge to him. For that reason he gave me a duplicate key so I could come in and out of here any time I wished. I didn't see any reason to tell Black Yankee about it — and I wouldn't be telling you only I'm leaving . . . Satisfied?'

'I guess so,' Thorn growled. 'Hurry up an' get your dress. I'll see you off the premises.'

She shrugged and turned away and he swung the torch beam round so that she could find her way amidst the tables. She vanished behind the screens which led to her dressing room at the rear of the 'orchestra' rostrum. After perhaps five minutes she returned with a large brown paper parcel under her arm.

Without a word Thorn saw her outside and then relocked the doors.

'Without wanting to seem *too* curious,' she said, 'what *were* you doing standing on that table?'

'None of your business.'

'Can't blame me for asking,' she shrugged. 'Good night . . . and, of course, good bye.'

Thorn caught her arm as she moved. 'Just a moment, kid. I know you don't like me — nor, I reckon, would I expect you to knowin' the kind of guy I am, but that doesn't stop me repeating my warning that you're takin' your life in your hands walking out of Twin Pines.'

'Which means you intend perhaps to shoot me in the back?'

'I never shot a woman anywheres

— an' I never shall, 'cept mebbe in self-defence.'

'I wish I could believe that, but I'm afraid I don't. You mean then that perhaps Black Yankee will get me?'

'He might — but he isn't the biggest danger. The danger'll come from the boys who used to work for him an' who are now workin' for me. You heard what I had to say in the saloon tonight, about any man or woman tippin' off the authorities as to what's going on in this town.'

'Certainly I heard — but I'm not telling the authorities anything. You can stew in your own beastly juice for all I care.'

'I've only your word for that — an' it's my policy not to trust words, only actions. When one of the boys sees you walkin' out of town tomorrow — as one of 'em surely will 'cos they're on the watch day and night — you're liable to get yourself tied up with some lead.'

For a moment or two the girl was silent, then she said contemptuously.

'It's surely up to you to prevent trouble of that sort, isn't it? You're the boss now. Tell the boys to lay off me.'

'I don't see why I should. You *might* tip-off the authorities at that!'

'I'll risk it!' the girl declared hotly. 'If only to show you what I think about you!'

'All right — but 'fore you do, start thinkin' how much safer you'd be goin' on as hostess with my guarantee that no man — not even myself — will molest you. Killer I may be, far as men are concerned. Wimmin are different. I've a code about 'em.'

'I hope I never hear what it is,' the girl retorted, and with quick, agitated movements she strode down the three steps and into the lamplighted street. Thorn watched her go, hugging her parcel tightly to her. At last she vanished in the region of the town's solitary hotel.

'Mebbe she'll think differently when she's cooled off a bit,' Thorn muttered; then his jaw tightening he removed from his pocket the bullet he had dug out of the saloon wall. Purposefully, he began walking, ending his journey at the somewhat ramshackle home of the mayor at the far end of the town.

He had to pound on the door with considerable force, and for quite a while, before a tubby figure in a night-shirt appeared, holding an oil lamp above his head.

'What in tarnation — ' He broke off and started, peering into the lampglow with his round eyes. 'Oh, it's you, Thorn! What gives?'

'You'll find out,' Thorn responded, and pushed roughly past into the small parlour. The mayor followed him in and set the lamp down on the table.

'Nice hour of night to come bustin' in,' the mayor complained. 'In fact I just don't understand you these days, Thorn. Never know you for the same lad who left town five years ago. You've changed a mighty lot. Your dad would have been plenty sick had he lived to see the heel you've turned into.'

'Yeah, mebbe he would,' Thorn admitted, a hard glitter in his agate-blue eyes in the lamplight. 'An' it's chiefly on account of him I'm here. I want to know just what happened to him. I've heard he was shot, but that isn't enough for me. By the law, as the mayor, you should have extracted the bullet and kept it in safe keeping until such time as you could let the authorities know that murder had been done, and so provide the evidence.'

'The law fell down dead as well as your old man,' Thorn, when Black Yankee came into town. I'd no chance to dig out any bullet — either from your father or Steve Bradshaw. Black Yankee was too smart. He had the bodies taken out to the mesa — an' that was that, I reckon. Y'know what it is out there. They'll never be found and in time the sand'll cover 'em.'

Thorn's eyes narrowed. 'So that was it, huh? Okay — who took the bodies there?'

'The guy called Lefty — one of the

five who goes around — or did go around — with Black Yankee. I reckon they're in thick with you now.'

'Lefty, eh? Thanks for the information. While I'm about it let me find out something else — Who actually shot my old man? As I figger it it might have been *any* of those outlaws.'

'Right,' the mayor agreed. 'They all fired at once. It's an old trick, so's nobody could actually prove who did the real killin' . . . '

'I'll stake what I've got that that guy called Jeff did it,' Thorn said slowly, clenching his fist. 'Tonight he demonstrated — after I'd challenged him — that he's the quickest trigger man in the outfit bar Yankee. I think Yankee might have let him do the shootin' rather than take the blame himself. Out of the wall I've dug the bullet Jeff fired tonight. I want to see if it matches the slug in my old man's body.'

The mayor raised an eyebrow questioningly.

'I don't get your angle, Thorn,' he

said. 'From the way you've been tellin'
I'd gotten it into my head that you just
don't care *what* happened to your old
man. Why this sudden interest in findin'
how he died an' who did it?'

'I'm sheriff now, aren't I?' Thorn
asked, shrugging. 'My job t' check up
on killings. When I've done it I'm not
goin' to tell the authorities for fear of
getting myself mixed up with 'em. I'll
be my own judge an' jury . . . You say
Steve Bradshaw was shot by Black
Yankee in self-defence?'

'That's right. Most anybody could
say it was that way.'

'Okay — then I'll go no further with
that. But I *will* try and check up on the
bullet in my old man — if I can find
him. That's up to Lefty. Thanks, Mayor
— I'll be seeing you.'

Without explaining further Thorn
departed. He walked perhaps quarter of
a mile along the boardwalk from the
mayor's house, then he paused and
stood thinking. Finally he made up his
mind, returned to Ma Brendick's

rooming house, and entered it silently by the night door at the side of the building. Without a sound he went up the stairs, pausing on the first corridor with its dim glimmer of gaslight, and looking along the silent vista. After a moment or two he moved cautiously forward, stopping again outside the door numbered 7.

'You there, Jeff?' he called, knocking lightly.

For a moment there was no answer and he had to repeat his question. Then there came sounds from within, the door latch clicked, and Thorn found himself gazing at a dim vision of a face.

'You, huh?' Jeff murmured. 'What the heck's the idea at this hour? Better come in . . . '

Thorn entered the dark room and waited. Jeff moved about; a match scraped, then the oil lamp was lighted. He stood revealed in a somewhat tattered pyjama suit, his sandy hair tousled.

'Sump'n wrong?' he questioned.

'That depends,' Thorn answered slowly. 'I've just had reason to talk to the mayor an' unless we're mighty careful it's possible he may start makin' trouble for us.'

'*That* little runt!'

'That doesn't count. He *is* the mayor — even more authority than I have as sheriff. He knows, I think, where the bodies of my old man and Steve Bradshaw are lyin', an' unless I'm dead wrong he's aiming at digging the bullets — or bullet — out of my old man and keeping it as evidence for later on. We've got to fix it so as he doesn't. If he finds somebody with a gun which fires bullets which *match* the ones in my old man, there'll be a necktie party for that person. I'm not takin' the risk. I don't think he's much concerned with Steve Bradshaw. Seems most people can prove Black Yankee shot him in self-defence, so there's no case as the law stands here. Different with my old man ... I s'pose you don't know who *did* shoot him?'

'Not for certain,' Jeff answered. 'Might ha' bin any of us — even me. All firin' at once y'can't tell . . . But if that's the sort of plan that old fool's got we've got to work fast.'

'Uh-huh — an' tonight too. I came here to find Lefty. It seems he took the bodies out to the mesa. Whereabouts is he in this joint?'

'Right next to this room. A coupla bangs on the wall'll bring him in quick. Want me to do that?'

Thorn nodded silently. Jeff turned to the wall, picked up his boot from the floor, and banged it twice on the faded wallpaper. There was a short interval, then after a hurried knock on the door Lefty came in, hastily scrambled into shirt, pants, and half boots. His general air of urgency abated somewhat as he saw the two men sitting waiting for him.

'What gives?' he questioned in surprise. 'What's all the excitement about? I thought you wus only going to bang the wall in case of emergency, Jeff?'

'This *is* an emergency,' Thorn told him steadily. 'We're going right now to dig a bullet, or bullets out of my old man's body — and you're leading the way.'

'What in heck do we want to do that for?' Lefty demanded.

Thorn gave him the details and the cowpuncher's expression changed slightly. He rubbed his chin.

'Yeah, that does sound as though it might work out mighty tough for somebody if we don't move quicker 'n the mayor. I reckon a simpler way would be to take care of the mayor. That's what Yankee would've done.'

'Mebbe so,' Thorn answered, 'but I'm runnin' this outfit now — not Yankee. And besides, takin' care of the mayor doesn't guarantee that he hasn't told others what he knows — an' by that I mean that he has discovered the location of the bodies. Our job is to move the bullets from my old man, then the mayor hasn't a thing to go on.'

'I don't quite understand how he ever *found* the bodies,' Jeff commented, frowning. 'Seems kinda strange — You hid 'em pretty well, Lefty, didn't you?'

'Sure did. Buried 'em in fact, in the sand. Only accident can have given the mayor the tip-off.'

'We're wastin' time,' Thorn decided, getting to his feet. 'Let's be on our way, Lefty. Your cayuse will be down with mine in the stable, I suppose?'

'Uh-huh.'

Thorn nodded and strode to the door. Jeff called after him.

'This mean you don't want me, then?'

'I reckon not,' Thorn told him. 'All I need is for Lefty to show me where the bodies are. I'll do the rest . . . Okay, Lefty, let's go.'

5

It was towards half-past four in the early hours when Thorn and Lefty rode back into town, their journey to the mesa over. It had been entirely successful, the solitary bullet which had killed his father now being in Thorn's pocket. He took leave of the cow-puncher outside the door of his bedroom, then stepped inside it and drew the catch.

Disregarding all thought of sleep Thorn lighted the lamp, pulled off his hat and kerchief and then settled himself on the bed edge, immediately under the lamplight. From his pockets he removed the bullet which had been in his father's body, and the one he had extracted from the wall of the saloon. A powerful pocket lens told him every-thing else he needed to know. Both bullets had plainly been fired by the same gun. They both had the same curious striker-pin markings on the cap; they were both the same calibre.

'Which, technically, makes Jeff the murderer of the old man,' Thorn mused, his eyes narrowed. 'That's mighty interestin' information — but the task is goin' to be how to use it. Have to be my own judge and executioner, I reckon — same as I'd planned at first.'

He sat for quite a time thinking the business out; then at last he sighed, put the two bullets away carefully in a corner of his shirt pocket and sewed them in place so no possible chance could dislodge them — then he meditated over further details.

'S'pose I'd better start gettin' busy with the printin' press next,' he muttered. 'After sayin' all that Benson'll be expecting it — and so will the boys if it comes to that. See what I can do tomorrow night . . . or rather tonight,' he corrected himself, watching the dawn greying the bedroom window.

His cogitations at an end he threw himself on the bed just as he was and slept soundly until breakfast time. It was towards half past nine when he left the rooming house, bound for the sheriff's office where he intended to take over his duties in all seriousness — if only as cover for his various other activities. He was half way there along the busy boardwalk when he found himself suddenly confronting Claire Henderson. He noticed at a glance that she was in a summery frock and a large lacy-brimmed hat — certainly not the kind of attire for going on a journey.

'So you took my advice,' he said, regarding her and giving a somewhat languid salute.

'Uh-huh.' The girl's grey-blue eyes studied him. 'I thought maybe I'd better when I came to think it over. This morning, from my bedroom window, I saw one or two of your boys knocking about — enough of them to make any escape on my part a somewhat uncomfortable experience.'

'I'm glad you're stayin',' Thorn said quietly. 'Just stick to your job as hostess and everythin'll be all right.'

'I've also another reason for staying, besides the possibility of it being awkward for me to get away,' the girl said.

'You have? You mean you kinda like Twin Pines?'

'Not since it became an outlaw town. No; my other reason is that you've started to interest me quite a lot.'

'Yeah?' Thorn gave a quick glance and then lounged back with his elbows on the boardwalk's tie rail. 'How come a killer has got you interested?'

'I'm wondering,' the girl said pensively, 'if you really *are* a killer. More I think about it, the more I doubt it.'

Thorn gave a grim smile. 'You take a lot of convincing, don't you? You saw what happened to that puncher last night when he had so much to say?'

'Oh yes, I saw all right — but it also occurred to me afterward that I'd never seen that particular man, or his friend who carried him out, before last night. Strangers are most uncommon in Twin Pines, and being hostess at the saloon I've come to know practically every face. Those two men were complete strangers to me — and it seems odd to me that the man who carried out the man you shot didn't come back.'

'Just the way of things,' Thorn responded, shrugging. 'And don't start goin' overboard for me, Miss Henderson. I'm not your type, any more than you're mine.'

Her grey-blue eyes were perfectly steady as she looked back at him.

'I'm not going overboard for you or anybody else — but there *is* a mystery about you, Mr Tanworth — and since I've more or less got to stay in Twin Pines I won't be happy until I've found out what it is. In the meantime, thanks for kicking out Black Yankee. I couldn't stand him at any price, but you're — er — much more tolerable.'

She gave a curious little smile and added, 'I'll be at the saloon tonight as usual, doing my job as hostess. I shan't run away now I realize how much you interest me.'

Thorn stared after her as she continued on her way along the boardwalk. His lips tightened and then relaxed again in a somewhat rueful smile. Thoughtfully he continued on his way to the sheriff's office, opened it up and passed inside. He had hardly thrown his hat on the peg and started examining the various papers connected with a sheriff's duties — which Black Yankee had apparently run in his own weird and wonderful way — before the door opened and Jeff came in. There was a certain look of menace about his sun-baked features.

'Look, Tanworth, am I supposed t' be your second-in-command?' he asked, curtly.

Thorn nodded. 'Sure you are. I told you that last night in the saloon, didn't I? Before everybody?'

'Yeah, but — You said you an' me would get together this mornin' to arrange plans for dealing with the cattle on neighbouring ranches. I've bin waiting for you to do that; then I heard from Ma Brendick that you'd walked outa the house. Now I find you here, all nice and cosy like a real genuine sheriff.'

'What makes you think I'm not?'

Jeff grinned sourly. 'Do I have to answer that? Bein' a sheriff is just a cover-up, so why pretend otherwise? What *I* don't like is being stood up. I want to know what you plan to do. Black Yankee would have fixed somethin' by now. You don't even seem to want to bother.'

'I'll fix something when I'm good and ready,' Thorn said, a glint in his agate-blue eyes. 'And in case you don't know it *I'm* the boss around here, and you're speakin' out of turn.'

'I reckon I'm entitled. I'm not just speakin' for myself — but for the rest of the boys as well. They want to know what sort of a boss you're goin' to be when you seem more interested in bein' sheriff than anythin' else.'

Thorn said briefly: 'The plans I'm layin' can't be worked out in five minutes. I'm going to spend today figgerin' things out. By tonight I'll have everythin' doped out and I'll tell you about it then — and the boys as well. In the Lucky Horseshoe.'

Jeff hesitated and then he nodded slowly.

'Okay . . . I'll tell the boys that. Save 'em getting restive.'

He turned away towards the door, then Thorn's voice made him pause again.

'Had you any particular grudge against my old man, Jeff, that led you to shoot him?'

The trigger-man turned and stared. '*Me* shoot him? Yore crazy! Black Yankee did that!'

'Think again, feller,' Thorn advised. 'Last night I dug the bullet out of my dad, and it matches the bullet you fired in the saloon . . . Don't get the idea wrong. Mebbe you shot my old man intentionally: mebbe not. The point I'm makin' is this. Don't start getting *too* tough in your demands on me, 'cos if you do I think those two bullets might find their way to the authorities, and I don't have to tell you what evidence like that would do to your chances of livin'.'

'You threatenin' me?' Jeff demanded fiercely.

'Warnin' you, more like it. I've got a hold over you, Jeff, and that makes me more sure that you'll do as you're told . . . Okay, you can blow now. You know where you stand.'

Jeff hesitated for several moments, then with a harshness about his thin-lipped mouth he turned and left the office. Thorn gave a grim smile to himself and went on studying the various papers and reports on the desk. In fact he spent all morning at it, combing the office from top to bottom and failing to discover anything interesting. Evidently Black Yankee had been careful enough not to leave anything in this particular office.

'Evidence — evidence — evidence,' Thorn muttered to himself at last. 'Sometimes wish a man could do without it. Reckon one could, as far as a guy like Black Yankee's concerned, but information of any sort helps.'

At noon he gave up his searching, left the office, and went down the street to Bill's Eating House. He thought a good deal over his lunch, then immediately after it paid a second visit to Josiah Benson. The old newspaper proprietor looked at him sourly as he entered.

'You again, huh?' he asked grimly. 'Well, what this time, son? Forget something last night?'

'I wasn't here last night, and you know I wasn't,' Thorn replied. 'Didn't find anything different to what you left it, did you?'

'Well, no. I just figgered that mebbe you'd been extra tidy or somethin'.'

'I'm here now to tell you that I shan't need your printing stuff after all,' Thorn said. 'Changed my plans.'

'Since you took over the town from Black Yankee, you mean?'

'Uh-huh! You heard about it, then?'

'I reckon there isn't anybody that ain't.' Benson came over from the hand press where he had been working and leaned his elbows on the counter, peering up into Thorn's expressionless face. 'Look, son, why don't you let your hair down? What are you tryin' to pull in this town? Yesterday, when you came in here with your hardware, you got me believin' for a while that you'd really gone to the bad. Now I've had time to think about it I reckon that . . . Well, I just don't believe it.'

'Why shouldn't you believe it?' Thorn snapped. 'I wouldn't be the first man to go to the bad, would I?'

'Nope — but I guess that if you were the outlaw you figger you are there'd be some mention from the authorities in Barville that they were on the prod for you — same as they are for Black Yankee. There'd be notices all over the territory. But there ain't any — and I'd

know about 'em if there was. I'm editin'
a paper, remember, an' it's my job to
know about such things.'

'All I can say is you must have missed
'em,' Thorn said with a shrug. 'And for
the moment I've nothin' more to say.
See you again — an' you can do what
you like with the printin' press — '

'As I like?' Benson interrupted.
'Meanin' what?'

'Meaning I shan't be wanting it.'

'Oh — that.' Benson looked disap-
pointed. 'I thought you meant I could
print what I see fit — like I usta before
Black Yankee put a stop to it.'

'So far as I'm concerned you can do
that too,' Thorn told him from the
doorway. 'Nothin' I'm doin' at the
moment that I'm afraid of you printing.
Later it may be different — when some
rustlin' starts f'rinstance.'

Benson gave a start. 'Darn it, lad,
you crazy enough to start stealin'
steers — ?'

'Why not? Some of the ranchers
around this district have got more'n

they need, and I could do with 'em — an' the money that goes with 'em. But you'll not print anythin' about that cos I reckon you'd have more sense.'

Benson was apparently going to say something more, but he did not get the opportunity for Thorn turned and left. Frowning to himself he went along the boardwalk and turned in again at the Lucky Horseshoe. At this time — early afternoon — there was not a soul in the place. The waiters and barkeep had cleaned everything up ready for the evening's 'performance' and to a great extent the fumes of the previous night's smoking had dispersed.

Thorn glanced about him once to make sure everything was shipshape, then he went across to the office and let himself in, taking care to turn the key in the lock behind him. Throwing off his hat he sat down at the roll-top and began pretty much the same investigation as in the sheriff's office — searching everything everywhere, and without coming upon a single thing that interested him.

In the end he gave it up, lighted a cigarette, and put his feet up on the desk. He remained more or less in his lounging position, dozing at intervals to catch up on the sleep he had lost in the night, until it came near time for the saloon to be opened up. Then he freshened himself up at the washbowl, brushed his hair before the cracked mirror, and went out into the saloon to open the doors.

Presently the barkeep arrived, and then the waiters. By the time they had got the lamps lighted, for little evening sunshine penetrated into the saloon's big rambling interior, Claire Henderson had come too, her coat thrown lightly over the backless top of her sequined evening gown, her fair hair catching the gleam of the lights. She paused in surprise as she beheld Thorn lounging at a corner table, smoking and musing.

'Early on the job tonight, Mr Tanworth,' she commented. 'Or have you been here some time, looking for the same thing you were looking for last night?'

Thorn glanced up at her. 'I found what I wanted last night — an' as for bein' here early why shouldn't I? Chief reason for it is to have a word with you before the place gets busy. Won't be an opportunity durin' the evening.'

'More instructions, I suppose?' The girl gave a sigh. 'Every boss I have seems to think up new ways for a hostess to behave. Why can't you leave me be? I'll do all right.'

'Sure you will,' Thorn agreed. 'Run it how you like; I'm satisfied. It's something else I want to ask — soon as you're ready.'

'Well, I — I can do it now.' The girl seated herself at the table, frowning slightly. 'What's on your mind?'

Thorn straightened up from his lounging position and kept his voice low.

'You told me this morning that you've become interested enough in me to stick around and see if you can find out somethin' about me. Okay — that's all right to me. But it works both ways. I've become interested in *you*, too. Chiefly because a gal like you just doesn't belong in an outlaw town. You wouldn't belong here even if it was *not* an outlaw town. Last night you as good as admitted that Black Yankee had a hold over you which kept you here ... Do you suppose you could tell me what that hold was? Or *is*, since he's still alive, I suppose, and may do anything at any moment.'

'It's no business of yours,' the girl said quietly.

'I think it may be. Black Yankee was kicked out of this town, remember. He won't be feelin' any too sweet towards anybody in it — especially towards those who he thinks he can perhaps injure. Suppose he gets nasty and you find yourself suddenly tied up with trouble? I could probably stop anythin' like that if I knew what was coming ... What have you done that gives

Black Yankee a grip on you?'

'I murdered a man back in Barville,' the girl said, biting her lip — and Thorn's eyes widened slightly.

'*You* did! Now I've heard everythin'.'

'It's true, I tell you!' Her voice was nervously exasperated at his obvious disbelief. 'There was a man called Rolf Peterson in Barville. He was in real estate and he advertised for a secretary. I answered and he interviewed me. He got fresh and — and there was a bit of a struggle. In the midst of it I made a grab at the desk, intending to pull something off it with which to hit him. Instead I caught hold of one of the drawers — I had my back to it at the time — and tugged it open. I saw a moment or two later there was a gun in the drawer . . . '

The girl paused, staring into the lamplight and empty saloon.

'So?' Thorn questioned.

'I — I whipped the revolver round and fired at him. Then I suppose the emotional strain or something got me down and I fainted. When I came to again he was lying dead beside me, blood on his shirt above the heart, and the gun was where it had dropped out of my hand to the floor. I — I made sure he was dead by taking his pulse. Then I panicked and ran for it . . . ' The girl's eyes went wide. 'Only I ran straight into a man who was in the corridor looking for an office number.'

'Black Yankee?' Thorn asked.

'Yes — but I didn't know it then. He looked a lot smarter then than recently. In riding outfit, of course, but it was pretty spruce and neat. He made me go back with him and look at the body — then he said something about being able to help me away from the law. I was scared of him and I refused his help. I said that I'd look after myself, that I knew of a quiet town — this one of Twin Pines — where I could go until the heat cooled off. So here I came . . . and Black Yankee followed. I got a pretty big shock when I realized how much of a killer and outlaw he really is.

I can't imagine how a man like him, on the run, could have the nerve to turn up in Barville to do some business with Peterson. That *was* his intention, by the way, until he realized I'd murdered the beast.'

'Mmmm . . . ' Thorn looked at the oil lamps casually, his expression giving nothing away. 'So that's the story, is it? Well, if he tries to hand on what he knows about you to the authorities I'll do what I can to help you . . . Thanks for being frank with me, Miss Henderson.'

'You could repay me by being as frank about yourself. From what I've heard from people in this town you never used to be a rough renegade. Seems you were generally liked. What's happened to change you?'

'Time's getting on,' Thorn told her, 'and the customers are coming in . . . You'd best be getting on with your job, hadn't you?'

She looked at him steadily, half in contempt and half in disappointment, then she got to her feet and left the table without another word. Thorn sat looking after her for a while, a pensive scowl on his grim features; then he rose too, went over to the bar, and ordered a whisky for himself.

For some time afterwards he remained silent, drinking and smoking by turns, his elbow on the counter, his gaze absently watching the saloon's habitués as they came trooping in. In the distance Claire Henderson presently reappeared and went about her usual duties — Then suddenly, amidst the buzz of conversation, rattle of poker chips and clink of glasses, there came an interruption. The batwing doors flew apart and a figure strode in, a gun levelled in each hand, the muzzles pointing straight at Thorn.

It was Black Yankee.

6

Thorn did not move a muscle as, amidst a sudden dead silence, the outlaw walked slowly across the saloon to the bar counter. He was filthy dirty from hard riding; a beard was sprouting incipiently around his heavy jowls. He did not look either left or right; his entire attention was focused on Thorn.

'Get 'em up, Tanworth!' he snapped.

Thorn obeyed, his lips tight as his guns were taken from him and tossed to a far corner behind the bar.

'Thought I'd gone, didn't yuh?' Yankee asked, grinning crookedly. 'Matter of fact I did go — part of the way along the trail. Then I suddenly stopped an' asked myself why? You bested me in that fight, sure — but there ain't nothin' to stop the loser comin' back again to recover his lost laurels.'

'And that is what you've decided to do?' Thorn asked calmly.

'Yeah. I set my heart on runnin' this town, Tanworth, and though I mebbe panicked at the time when you licked me I've got my senses back now. You an' me is goin' to settle this business of leadership once an' for all.'

Thorn shrugged. 'Okay. Mind if I finish my drink?'

'Go ahead — but don't throw it in my face if you want to keep healthy! An' give me a double brandy,' Yankee added to the barkeep.

In another moment it was forthcoming and both men drank slowly, watching each other as narrowly as a couple of prairie dogs coveting an identical titbit. Then Thorn's eyes lowered to Yankee's right-hand gun. He had placed the left-hand one on the counter so he could handle his glass of brandy.

'Figgerin' to shoot me an' get it over with?' Thorn asked.

'Can you think of a good reason why I shouldn't?'

'Only that it isn't fightin' clean to shoot a man when you've thrown away his hardware. Not that I expect you to know anything about clean shootin' though.'

'Get this, Tanworth,' Yankee said deliberately, putting down his empty glass. 'I've come back into town to take *care* of you. I don't care *how* I do it, see? Just as long as you're carried out with your boots on when I'm through. I owe you plenty — an' now you're going to get it.'

The gun levelled; there was the faint hair-thin sound of the trigger drawing back. Simultaneously, Thorn kicked out his right foot violently and it cracked across the outlaw's shin. He gave a howl of sudden anguish and his gun aim deflected. The bullet landed in the mirror over the back-bar and split it in five tinkling, crumbling javelins.

'Okay, you asked for it,' Thorn said, and his left lashed out. Yankee jerked his head out of the way of it, too late to realize it had been a feint. Instead he put himself in line with a smashing right-hander which knocked him flying into the midst of the piled-up bottles on the counter. Even as he floundered amidst them Thorn dived, tore his gun from his hand and hurled it across the saloon. The gun on the counter he flung in the opposite direction — then he stood ready and waiting, his big fists doubled.

Panting, Black Yankee remained where he was for the moment. The reason became apparent in a second or two. Jerking up, it became obvious that he had a large whisky bottle in his hand, his fingers gripping the neck. Savagely he smashed the bottle over the edge of the counter, the spirit flooding round his feet. The remaining section with its needle-sharp teeth remained in his hand, gleaming in the light.

'More'n one way of dealing with a polecat like you, Tanworth, I reckon,' he muttered — then he dived.

Thorn waited until the last second, then as the frightful gouging weapon swung down venomously towards his face he doubled up, ramming his head with savage violence into Yankee's stomach. Stopped dead in his rush, every scrap of wind blasted right out of him by the impact, he dropped the bottle top. He was lifted off his feet, still with Thorn's head rammed into his middle, and then he found himself flung violently backwards. With a devastating crash he dropped amidst the nearest tables, pulling them over on top of him, beer, cards and chips tumbling into his face.

Taking advantage of the second's lull Thorn swung round, picked up the bottle top, and threw it far out of reach — then he returned to deliver an uppercut as Yankee struggled to his feet. Thorn miscalculated, however. Yankee's boot came up and the heavy toe struck Thorn clean in the throat. Gulping, his head exploding with fire, he reeled backwards and landed flat on his back in front of the bar. For the moment he could not speak or hardly breathe, and with it went his earlier initiative.

Yankee was upon him instantly, forcing one hand up excruciatingly behind his back, whilst his free hand crushed murderously into Thorn's already agonizing throat. Thus pinned Thorn could scarcely move, and with every moment he could feel his attempts to breathe becoming more and more intolerable.

With a subconscious effort Thorn moved his free left hand from under his body and brought it upwards and backwards in an effort to seize the outlaw crushing down upon him. He failed, and the strangling pressure on his throat grew ever tighter — Thorn's vision began to blur. He felt sure his eyes were going to explode. Through the haze he saw a girl's feet and the glitter of sequins on her gown — then, almost magically as it seemed to him, a gun was in his hand.

With his last ounce of effort he twisted his body slightly and brought the gun from beneath him. He fired, and the pinning weight suddenly became even heavier. But the strain upon his throat relaxed gently and he could breathe again. He lay motionless, the fumes of the gun muzzle coiling round his nostrils.

There seemed to him to be a long, ominous silence — then voices began speaking; feet began moving. The load was pulled from him and he was dragged to his feet. He looked about him, swaying dizzily, conscious of the gun in his hand and the sprawled figure of Black Yankee.

'I reckon that settles it,' Jeff said bitterly, glancing up from a quick examination of the outlaw. 'Yankee's dead.'

'But it isn't murder,' Claire Henderson said quickly. 'It was self-defence. It was Yankee or — or Tanworth for it. Yankee'd have killed him if I hadn't given Tanworth a gun to protect himself.'

Jeff scowled. 'Mighty keen on makin' sure this sheriff of ours didn't get rubbed out, ain't you?'

'Yankee took an unfair advantage and deserved all he got,' the girl retorted. 'Any clean fighter would have waited for his opponent to get over that blow in the throat.'

'Yeah — right enough,' murmured somebody, and there was a general murmur of assent, except from the five who had been Black Yankee's closest followers.

Thorn looked at the girl curiously, frowned a little to himself, and then holstered the gun he was holding. Without a word he picked up its twin and shoved it in the opposite holster. Then he looked about him on the assembly and motioned to the mayor in the near foreground. He came forward immediately.

'You saw what happened, Mayor,' Thorn said. 'What would you call it?

Murder — or self-defence?'

'Self-defence. Ain't no doubt about it.'

'Okay; then that settles it. We'll strip the body of its possessions for you to keep a record of it, Mayor — along with his guns; then at the proper time you can turn in the facts to the authorities in Barville if they ever need 'em. I'll give you a hand to carry him to your home and strip him.'

The mayor nodded, motioned to two nearby cowpunchers, and with Thorn assisting as well the body was lifted and carried out of the saloon. At the batwings Thorn paused for a moment and hurried back for the outlaw's guns, lying behind the bar. As he passed the silent Claire Henderson he gripped her arm momentarily.

'Thanks a lot,' he murmured. 'I reckon you saved my life — an' I shan't forget it.'

Before she could comment he had hurried out after the mayor and cowpunchers, and between them they bore their burden down the street. Back in the saloon Claire Henderson stood thinking for a moment or two; then making up her mind she went to her dressing room and reappeared in a moment or two in her overcoat. Without a word of explanation to the barkeep or the waiters she left the saloon, crossed the road, and presently entered Ma Brendick's boarding house. Ma Brendick herself, eighteen stone of good nature, was in the hall lighting the oil lamps.

'Oh, Miss Henderson!' she exclaimed, blowing out the taper and coming forward. 'I've seen you knocking about the town — what's the trouble? Wanting a room?'

'No, thanks, Ma. But I would like to go up to Mr Tanworth's room and wait for him coming in. I don't think he'll be very long.'

'Wait for him coming in?' Ma Brendick stared. 'But why d'you want to do that? Can't you find him in the town and talk to him? Shouldn't be difficult.'

Claire smiled faintly. 'More difficult than you think. He's with the mayor, attending to a dead body. Black Yankee's.'

'Black Yankee's! You mean somebody got that skunk in the finish?'

'Uh-hah. Mr Tanworth himself.'

''Bout time,' Ma Brendick muttered. 'We'd have been headin' for plenty of trouble before we'd finished if that critter had kept on roamin' around . . .' She reverted suddenly to the question at hand. 'Okay, dearie, go up to his room if you want. It's number three first floor . . . Mmm — so Black Yankee's dead, is he? That means I've got his room empty again. Good job. He never paid a cent.'

Leaving the woman smouldering with indignation Claire went up the staircase and along the corridor. Room 3 was not locked. She opened the door and went into the twilight, seating herself at the window to wait. As she sat she looked at the object she had brought with her in her palm — a

114

small, gleaming badge. The more she studied it, the more she smiled . . . then presently, at the sound of feet along the corridor, she hastily hid it again and got to her feet.

Thorn came into the room in the dim light. He looked at the girl without any evidence of surprise, then turned to the oil lamp and lighted it. As he blew the match out he gave a nod.

'Howdy, Miss Henderson. Ma told me you were here . . . Glad you are. I'd not only like to thank you again for saving my life in the Lucky Horseshoe, but I've got some information which I think will interest you.'

'I might say the same,' Claire said quietly. 'Perhaps I'd better say my piece before you say yours.'

'Okay,' Thorn agreed, tossing down his hat and perching on the edge of the table. 'Ladies first, I reckon.'

The girl extended her hand, palm upward.

'This is yours,' she said, her voice low. 'It fell out of your pocket whilst

Black Yankee had you on the floor. I thought you'd want it back.'

Thorn took the badge from her and gave a little start. Then his hard grin changed slowly and became a rueful smile.

'Which about finishes everything,' he sighed. 'I should have been more careful . . . Anybody else see this?'

'No. I saw it fall and nobody else had a chance to glimpse what it was . . . It makes a tremendous difference, Mr Tanworth, to know that you're a US Marshal and not a killer. It explains a lot of things too — your queer behaviour at times; the way folks here have not been able to credit your hard-boiled pose. It might even explain your standing on the table examining the saloon wall.'

Thorn nodded. 'Sit down, Miss Henderson. It's pretty plain I've one or two things to explain. In a way I'm glad this happened. To you, at least, I don't have to pretend any more to be a cut-throat on the lines of Black Yankee.'

'No, not any more,' Claire agreed, all the cold anger gone from her pretty face. 'In some ways this isn't such a terrific surprise, Mr Tanworth. Instinctively I felt you were *not* in the same class as Black Yankee.'

'I'm playing a pretty dangerous game all on my own,' Thorn told her seriously. 'When my dad sent me away from town to become a man I decided he might be right — so I joined the police. I did well enough to become a marshal in five years and not so long ago I was instructed to find Black Yankee, a notorious outlaw, and his gang — and bring them in. I traced him as far as Barville where, I found, he was planning a particularly audacious land swindle with a man named Rolf Peterson.'

'Peterson!' the girl ejaculated. 'The man I shot!'

'Peterson anyway,' Thorn replied ambiguously. 'Unfortunately for me I was a step or two behind Yankee and Peterson was dead when I caught up with him. But I trailed Yankee and his boys as far as Twin Pines here. I knew I couldn't do much without getting on the inside — so I came into town as a killer and outlaw, using my father's throwing me out as an excuse for my having gone to the bad. I spat on his memory, much though it hurt me, to provide the necessary conviction. I also convinced Black Yankee I was a top-line forger — simply by showing him genuine dollar bills which he mistook for forgeries of exquisite craftsmanship. In a word, I did everything I could to make believe I was a low-down, same as Yankee . . . '

'Then?' Claire asked quietly.

'Well, I found I couldn't get all the evidence I needed on Black Yankee unless I became the boss in his place — and I had to do it *quickly*, so as not to give him the chance to clear away any evidence he might have either in the sheriff's office or the saloon office. However, I didn't find anything . . . Turning him adrift was the only thing I could do for the moment, but I felt pretty sure one or other of the boys watching for him would nail him and take him in to Barville on suspicion. Evidently he was too smart for them for he turned up here again . . . I couldn't arrest him without giving myself away, and I want the whole *gang*, not just him alone.'

'What boys do you mean would be watching for him?' Claire asked.

Thorn grinned. 'The one I shot 'dead' and the guy who carried him out. You came pretty near it when you said you'd never seen them before. You were right. They were marshals, same as me, planted.'

'You — you mean — ?'

'All part of the act. They came into town by cover of night. The argument was all a put-up job. I fired blanks and the chap who got killed — apparently — had only to dye his shirt as he clapped his hand to his chest. His pal took care nobody else got near enough to find it was a fake. Their job then was to stay on watch for Black Yankee being thrown out of town. I don't know what happened. Mebbe he was too quick for them and shot them. I'll only find that out when I next get in touch with headquarters. So, right now, I've the rest of the gang to rope in. Jeff comes next. I've got the necessary evidence to show that he murdered my old man.'

'A dangerous game,' Claire said, 'is right! If once one of those trigger-men suspects, your life won't be worth two buttons.'

'I know; but none of them *can* suspect unless you say something, and I'm pretty sure you won't. As for my badge I'll take better care of it henceforth — stitch it into my shirt, same as I have with the two bullets for evidence.' Thorn brisked up a little and continued. 'Anyway, the first part of my job is finished. Black Yankee is dead, and the Rolf Peterson murder is cleared up. You didn't do it, so forget about it.'

'But I thought — '

'I never did, in spite of your story

— and now I've got the proof of it. In going through Black Yankee's belongings I found a small diary, just the kind of thing an egoist like Yankee *would* carry around. Without going into the details, it shows clearly how the Peterson murder was committed, and that he committed it. It seems he was about to climb through the window of the office to shoot Peterson when he saw you there, a revolver in your hand, just sinking to the floor in a faint. At that moment Peterson was staring at you, but he was very much alive. Apparently Yankee then shot Peterson point blank with the gun *you* had used — so as to be sure the bullet from that gun would go in Peterson. Yankee then wiped the gun clean and pressed your unconscious hand upon it to provide fingerprints. That done, he went out into the corridor to wait for you coming out. In other words, he shot Peterson just as he had intended, but switched the blame to you. This, he intended — still according to his diary — to use as a lever for keeping a hold over you. I'll spare you the lustful details he wrote in his diary. But you queered his pitch somewhat by refusing his aid and heading for Twin Pines. And that, I reckon, is the whole story. Peterson and Yankee had been co-partners and yet sworn enemies for long enough — both of them chisellers and mixed up in illegal land grabbings. Yankee, deciding not to risk staying in Barville with you, his hoped-for stooge, on the way to Twin Pines, followed you. The rest you know.'

'And the relief is something I just can't describe,' the girl breathed, her eyes shining. 'I didn't *think* I shot Peterson, but I could never be sure. That was why I had to make up to that — that beast of a Yankee.'

'The evidence I have puts you in the clear,' Thorn smiled; 'but it doesn't end my troubles by a long way. I've the rest of the gang to clean up. I can indict Jeff for the murder of my father — but I'll have to do it carefully, otherwise the rest of the boys will suspect and I'll find lead in me before I know it. The remainder of the boys I want to nab red-handed when they are actually engaged in cattle rustling — and that'll take a bit of planning. But if I can do it I'll have them with the goods on 'em and that will be that. Which is why I've had so much to say about organizing raids on the neighbouring ranches. By tomorrow I should have things mapped out — then I'll have to go to headquarters and notify them what I'm driving at. Also have them send the necessary men to make the clean-up at the spot I select. Everything,' Thorn finished, 'depends on the fact that none of them get the vaguest hint of my real status before I have a chance to nail 'em.'

'How do you propose letting your headquarters know?' Claire asked. 'Won't be safe to trust the telegraph, will it?'

'I'll go personally to Barville, under cover of night when nobody can see me. It's the only way.'

'I see ... If you ask me, Mr Tanworth, your biggest danger will come from that man Jeff. He's got more brains than the rest of those gunmen and I've more than an idea that he already suspects something somewhere. I think he rather wondered at my giving you a gun with which to save yourself tonight. I did that, by the way, when I realized from your fallen badge that you're a marshal.'

'Yes, Jeff's a tough customer all right,' Thorn agreed, frowning, 'and a born killer. Once I get him behind bars the rest of the boys won't be difficult. I can only hope he doesn't really suspect as much as he appears to.'

The girl sat musing for a while, then she got to her feet and held out her hand.

'You'll — forgive all the things I said about you?'

'Of course,' Thorn smiled. 'They were quite a tribute to my acting, come to think of it.'

'What do you want me to do to help you?'

'Just as you are doing — and maintain your contempt whenever we meet in public. Nobody, not even the mayor, knows what I'm really getting at. It's entirely our secret. Tomorrow,' Thorn finished, 'I'll help the mayor to bury Yankee's body in the desert — the usual disposal assigned to an outlaw — then I'll see what I can do tomorrow evening to get the boys to agree to a rustling raid. I'll do it in the saloon where everybody can hear me. That ought to make it convincing.'

'I'll co-operate to the end,' Claire said quietly. 'There's one thing, though. When I came here I found your door unlocked. Do you think that's altogether wise with these trigger-men living in the same rooming house?'

'It's psychology,' Thorn smiled. 'If I leave the room unlocked they'll be pretty well convinced that I can't have anything worth hiding, and trust me all the more because of it. Naturally, any evidence I might have of being a marshal is *not* in this room. I carry it with me — like the badge. Thanks for the tip, though.'

'Just a thought — Thorn,' Claire smiled.

'That's better! Much less formal. No objections to my calling you Claire, I suppose?'

'None.' The girl gripped Thorn's outstretched hand. Then with a friendly smile she was gone and Thorn slowly closed the door.

7

When Claire returned to her hotel towards noon the following morning, after her usual trip to the Lucky Horseshoe to make preparations for her evening's work as hostess, she was surprised to find Jeff, the late Black Yankee's best trigger-man, lounging at the foot of the three steps which led to the entrance. His horse was secured to the tie rack and he watched the girl narrowly as she came up.

Claire made to avoid him, but his hand reached out suddenly and gripped her arm with painful tightness.

'I want a word with you, Miss Henderson,' he said briefly. 'Get inside the buildin', to your room, and don't make any fuss if y'know what's good for you.'

'Do you think you can — ' Claire stopped, realizing that in the pocket of the short jacket Jeff was wearing — a most unusual circumstance — he was cocking a revolver. Her eyes moved back to his grim, swarthy face.

'I ain't kiddin',' he said coldly. 'Go on — keep movin'. An' if the hotel manager has anythin' to say, use your wits — but fast!'

Cornered, Claire appreciated that there was nothing she could do. Her heart beating a little faster, she entered the hotel's main hallway, fully determined to give some sign or other to one of the staff, and risk the gun, but as circumstances had it there was nobody in sight. She headed for the lift until Jeff made her turn off and go up the stairs. When at last she entered her room on the first floor with Jeff immediately behind her she swung round angrily.

'What's the idea of this, anyway?' she demanded. 'What do you want with me?'

'Information — no more, no less,' Jeff replied, and turned the key in the lock. Then he put his gun back in its holster and stood looking at her. She backed away towards the half-open window, down which the shade was half drawn to shield the pitiless glare of the sun, and stood waiting.

'I've got plenty of reason for thinkin' you an' that guy Thorn Tanworth are playin' some sort of game together,' Jeff said at last, sitting on the edge of the bed and cuffing his hat up on his forehead.

'Game?' What on earth are you talking about?'

'You probably think I'm a mug,' Jeff said sourly. 'Mebbe Tanworth thinks I am too — but you're both wrong. I'm a smart guy. Smart enough to notice things.'

Claire did not say anything. Her mouth was dry. She was locked in the room with a merciless killer — and knew it.

'I've bin thinkin',' Jeff continued. 'There wus somethin' mighty queer about you suddenly decidin' to slip Tanworth that hardware in the saloon last night when things was goin' badly fur Yankee. Why'd you do it? Fust time you've ever shown any real interest in Tanworth. Must ha' bin a reason. From the way you've behaved up to then anybody would think you'd ha' bin glad to see Tanworth rubbed out.'

'If anybody had to be rubbed out I preferred it to be Yankee!' Claire retorted.

'Yeah. Which to my way of thinkin' means that you thought Tanworth wus *worth* savin'. Why?'

Claire did not reply.

'I said *why?*' the gunman blazed at her. 'An' what wus your reason for hangin' around Ma Brendick's roomin' house last night 'til Tanworth came in? I saw you go in — an' I saw you come out. I watched you ever since you gave him that gun in the saloon . . . You've got some reason for stickin' beside him, sister, and by hell I mean to find out what it is.'

'Are you going to get out of here

— or do I call the manager?' Claire demanded.

'Manager?' Jeff grinned. 'Don't make me laugh! You go anywhere near that bell-push an' I'll blast you out from under that nice hair of yourn.' His grin died suddenly and he got to his feet. Reaching out he gripped the girl's wrist tightly and forced her arm so savagely up her back she dropped, gasping to her knees.

'Now, start talkin'!' he ordered. 'That guy Tanworth isn't all he seems to be: I'll swear it. I never did think so — and I've thought so still less since he rubbed out Black Yankee. You're in with him, whatever it is. Better start talkin' afore I break your arm.'

Claire gave a desperate tug, but it only served to make Jeff grip her wrist all the tighter. At the same time he increased the pressure, and so intense was the pain tears started into her eyes.

'Don't make no difference to me how long I keep this up,' Jeff explained. 'I want to know the truth about Tanworth so I know how I stand. Talk, damn you!' he exploded, and Claire gave a smothered scream at the tearing pain which belted through her.

'All — all right. I'll tell you,' she choked. 'He's — he's a marshal and — '

'Yeah, a marshal,' agreed a voice through the partly open lower window.

Jeff wheeled round, his hand flying to his gun, but he was not quick enough. Thorn, half in the room, lashed out the toe of his boot and it hit the gunman in the mouth. His lower lip suddenly streaming blood, he reeled back across the room, hit the bed, and fell across it. Immediately Thorn finished his entry into the room, dived across at the gunman, and whirled him up. Savagely, mercilessly, he rained blows into his face and across the back of his head, battering him clean across the room until he crashed helplessly into a corner and lay motionless, blood still flowing from his cut lip.

For a moment or two Thorn stood

looking at him, then he turned to the girl.

'Seems like I came at the right moment,' he commented. 'I happened to notice Jeff's horse outside the hotel — just as I was passing on my way to Ma Brendick's. I couldn't think of anybody else except you who he'd be wantin' to see. So I found out the way — vaultin' up on to the veranda roof below. Pity he knows so much,' Thorn finished grimly. 'I'm left no choice now but to run him in. Lock him up in the cell back of the sheriff's office until the authorities can come from Barville and take him.'

The girl rubbed her aching arm painfully. 'I just wouldn't have told him that much only I just couldn't stand more of that punishment — '

'Okay, okay, forget it,' Thorn murmured. 'Simply means I'll have to alter my plans a bit, that's all — '

He broke off, wheeled, and flung the girl down flat as a bullet whanged through the air over their heads and plugged itself in the wall. In the corner Jeff lay crouched, dabbing his cut lip with one hand and holding his gun in the other.

'If you think yore runnin' me in, Tanworth, yore crazier than I figgered,' he breathed, scrambling to his feet. 'I'm takin' care of you right now — an' this gal — '

Thorn had not a second to lose. He grabbed the rug edge and pulled. It did not overbalance the outlaw but it made him stagger exactly at the second he fired his gun. The bullet went wide and not two seconds later a hammer blow under the chin hurled him across the room. Too late to save himself, he toppled backwards through the open window, slid down the sloping veranda roof outside and vanished.

'Bad move on my part, that,' Thorn panted, scrambling through the window quickly. 'That gives him the chance to get away — '

He broke off, relaxing. It was too late to do anything. Jeff was already astride his horse, spurring it up the main street as fast as it would go. Thorn looked after him for a moment or two, then he slowly withdrew into the room again.

'That settles that, I reckon,' he sighed, giving the girl a grim look.

'And all my fault!' The distress she felt was obvious. 'But for my — '

'No fault of yours, Claire. I keep tellin' you that. The fault was mine for knockin' him through the window. Only part I don't like is him knowing that I'm a marshal. If he comes back into town and tells the rest of the boys all my plans will fall to bits. The only thing against that is that he won't risk it for fear of my having a trap baited for him. If he hits the trail, as he seems likely for doing, he'll be picked up — sooner or later.'

The girl waited as he stood thinking; then at last he seemed to come to a decision. He gave a shrug.

'Nothing I can do except go right ahead as I'd intended,' he said. 'Tonight I'll be telling the boys about the rustlin' plan. Since Jeff won't be there I'll make sure of the fact by saying he's gone on ahead to arrange things. That'll lend even more conviction. If the boys agree to my plan I'll ride over to Barville during the night and get help — enough anyway to rope in this lot of cut-throats the minute they start to attack the ranch I have in mind.'

'When do you propose bringing this raid off?' the girl asked.

'Tomorrow night. It'll take me all tonight to get to Barville and back. It's a considerable distance, remember — one heck of a round trip.'

'Anything I can do?'

Thorn smiled. 'Only go on being hostess — an' look as though you hate me like poison.'

'That,' Claire said, 'is going to be difficult . . . hating you I mean.'

Thorn smiled but did not say anything. He unlocked the door and then departed.

★ ★ ★

For the remainder of the day Thorn was jumpy — not from fear but because the thought of Jeff returning formed such a danger to his plans. Apparently, though, the outlaw had left town — and stayed gone. Certainly there was no visible sign of him. Thorn could not be blamed for failing to notice a figure on the roof of the livery stable, almost concealed by the somewhat crazy flue-chimney jutting into the air. Jeff, in fact, had not gone very far and was deeply interested in all that was going on, uncomfortable through his position was in the relentless blaze of the sun.

It was just after sundown when Thorn entered the Lucky Horseshoe. A glance satisfied him that all the men he wanted to harangue were present. Claire, too, was there, but maintaining her act she turned away in apparent disgust as Thorn glanced at her across the smoke-filled room.

The eyes of the punchers and some of the women with whom they were talking followed Thorn's movement from batwings to bar counter. He ordered a drink, swallowed it, and then turned with a look of decision in his eyes.

'Well, you guys, everything's fixed,' he said, and looked about him to see the effect. 'You'll have noticed Jeff isn't here. That's because he's gone on ahead to make some advance preparations. Tomorrow night we're cleaning up the Double-S ranch north of here, an' if we're smart there's some two hundred head of cattle we can clean up as well.'

'Now yore talkin',' commented Lefty, rolling himself a cigarette. 'That's what we've bin waitin' for — some action.'

'I know; but these things take workin' out,' Thorn told him. 'Everything's set now — except for my knowin' how many of you are goin' to be in on this raid. Before you make up your minds don't forget that there'll be a sizeable packet for each one of you out of the cattle deal.'

The men turned and murmured among themselves, then presently

138

hands began to rise. The four men who were known trigger-men were the first to assent, and the number grew until there were twenty. Thorn surveyed the hands and gave a grim smile.

'Okay — that looks healthy enough to me. And the rest of you are thinkin' what bad boys we are, huh?'

'Not much doubt of it, is there?' Claire Henderson asked, with studied bitterness. 'What beats me is that you have the barefaced gall to stand there and arrange a rustling raid — and maybe even murder — with most of the town's inhabitants listening. What's to stop one of us giving them the tip-off at the Double-S and ruining all your plans?'

'Jeff's on guard near the Double-S, and there isn't a man or woman breathing that can get near that spread to give warning without being seen. As for the law, its nearest base is in Barville — scores of miles away, an' I've guarded *that* route too, so the luck wouldn't be any better. I reckon I don't need to add that nobody stands a chance of using the telegraph. Believe me, I've got this game sewn up tight.'

The girl turned away with a gesture of contempt and Thorn gave a sardonic grin. He turned his attention back to the men.

'Here's the plan,' he said. 'We muster at the fork road north of the trail at midnight — be plenty dark enough then; then we bear down on the Double-S in force. If there's trouble from Seth Calloway who runs the spread he'll be taken care of pronto. There will also be his outfit to watch out for; they live in the bunkhouse but I reckon we can shoot fast enough to take care of them too — '

'Y'mean wipe 'em out?' Lefty demanded, and Thorn glared at him.

'Any reason why not? You gettin' soft in your old age?'

'Like heck I am. I was only thinkin' we'll have around a dozen men to deal with, all of 'em pretty fast shooters.'

'Twenty of us here, aren't there? If twenty can't eliminate twelve there's something mighty wrong. Fact remains, Lefty — an' it applies to all of you — we're not goin' to stand arguin' once we get to the Double-S. We shoot first — an' no questions. That understood?'

'Okay,' Lefty agreed, who had apparently made himself foreman. 'Then what happens?'

'We turn loose around two hundred head of cattle. I know there are plenty more steers than that, but we couldn't handle 'em in the dark and in the narrow valley way; so two hundred'll be quite enough. Once we've got them into the valley we drive them out at the narrow end and from there on I'll tell you what to do. It will depend on how things work out. I'm arrangin' for a bunch o' boys to come over and collect the steers we give 'em.' Thorn put his hands on his hips and looked aggressively about him. 'Anything you guys want to say about that?'

There was silence. The answer

141

comprised nods of agreement from the men who were willing to join the raid, and looks of contempt from those who were holding off.

'All right, that's settled,' Thorn said. 'Miss Henderson — come here a minute.'

The girl turned in surprise. 'What do you want *me* for?'

'You're supposed to be hostess around here, aren't you?' Thorn asked her coldly. 'I want to give you the key to lock the place up when it's closing time. I'm leaving: I've got things to work out.'

She shrugged and came over to him. Visibly, with so many eyes upon them, he gave her the key and added in an undertone,

'Look after yourself, kid. I'm heading for Barville right away to tell them the plan's laid. If this works out as I hope it should these bright boys will run right into a trap tomorrow night.'

Looking back at the assembled men, he added in his normal voice,

'I'm quittin' now, boys — goin' back

to my room to work out some details, an' I may ride over later and check with Jeff. I'll see you tomorrow morning — in here — to fix the final arguments. Okay?'

'Okay,' Lefty confirmed; and with a nod Thorn took his departure.

Nobody said anything for a moment or two — then gradually the evening's business drifted back into its normal routine. Claire shifted position — put away the key in the small pocket of her dress belt and returned to her usual task of perambulating in and out of the tables, seeing to it that the customers were being looked after by the waiters. The three-piece 'orchestra' struck up a tune; the poker chips began to rattle.

In her mind's eye, as she continued walking about, Claire had a vision of Thorn riding hard through the night, bound for Barville and his headquarters. She smiled to herself. The mental vision of him racing under the stars and through the night wind was a pleasant one. She wondered if his emotions towards her were similar to hers towards him . . .

Then, suddenly, all her speculations and thoughts crumbled. In glancing towards the batwings she registered a discovery that suddenly set her heart racing . . . Jeff was coming into the saloon, hands on the butts of his guns, his swarthy face grimly earnest.

Claire hesitated, half turned, and then stopped. Had she been a little further towards the end of the saloon she could have slipped safely away. But not as things were. Jeff had already seen her.

'Over here, sister,' he ordered briefly, pointing a finger down significantly in front of himself.

Claire glanced about her and met curious looks. She set her face and walked towards the bar counter, just as Lefty did the same thing.

'What gives?' Lefty asked, puzzled. 'I thought you wus over at the Double-S spread on guard.'

'Yeah — that's what you was meant

to think, I reckon,' Jeff responded. 'But I'm here, ain't I? I'll tell you about it in a minnit. How many boys here are followin' out Thorn Tanworth's orders?'

'About a score of us. Why?'

'Get 'em all together. I've things to tell yuh. Go on — quick!'

Lefty still looked surprised but he turned away to follow out instructions. Since Jeff had returned he was more or less a deputy-boss, much though Lefty personally disliked the idea.

'As fer you — ' Jeff's malignant eyes turned to Claire. 'I'm aimin' to fix you, sister, so's you can't talk outa turn. I guess I should rub you out, but I'll come to that later. Too many witnesses right now, an' that ain't my policy. Get goin' into that office back there!'

Claire hesitated, then Jeff's voice breathed in her ear.

'You particularly *like* havin' your arm twisted, or are you goin' to do as yore told?'

Claire had no choice. Turning, she walked past the bar and to the office door. Jeff threw it open for her and followed her in. He kicked the door shut behind him. For a moment or two there was dim gloom, only relieved by the light gleaming through the glass fanlight at the top of the door. Jeff ignited the oil lamp and then dropped the match at his feet and trod on it. Throughout the entire performance Claire kept her eyes on him, trying to conceal the terror she felt. Deep down she was infinitely more frightened of Jeff than she had ever been of Black Yankee. There were vicious, lustful depths in this sadistic killer from which she instinctively recoiled.

'I'd like t'deal with you properly, but I ain't got time,' Jeff said finally. 'So I'll take care of you until I come back and finish things. I ain't aimin' to kill you — not yet least-ways. You an' me are goin' to have fun together afore I do that. Right now I'm tyin' you up good an' hard — and the rest'll come later on.'

He flung out his hand, gave her a shove, and she collapsed in the swivel chair at the desk. Tearing away the cord from the drawn shade, Jeff bound it tightly round her arms, dragging them behind her and triple knotting them to the chair. He searched round until he found a piece of string, which took care of her ankles. A piece of blotting paper thrust in her mouth and held in place with deed-tape, wrapped round four times, completed the job. Hardly able to breathe and utterly pinned to the chair, Claire could only gaze in fear, wondering what was going to happen next. As she did so, Jeff surveyed her critically.

'Yeah — reckon you'll do like that 'til I come back,' he said. 'I may be some time since I've got your boyfriend to take care of — but we'll make up for it when I *do* return, huh?'

He grinned and then blew out the oil lamp. The key rattled in the lock as he turned it. It rattled again when he was on the other side of the door, then Claire was left in the dim reflected glow from the saloon beyond.

8

Returning to the saloon, Jeff looked about him — first at the knot of a score of men whom Lefty had gathered together — then at the main body of customers watching interestedly. Jeff scowled at them and then spoke briefly.

'Place is closin',' he announced. And at the roar of protest, he added, 'Yeah, yeah, I know it's an hour an' a half afore closing time, but it's the boss's orders. I reckon we've t'do as he says. Miss Henderson's already gone home . . . or leastways to her hotel. Get movin', the lot of you!'

'Me too?' asked the barkeep in surprise, and looked suspiciously towards the nearby office. Knowing the place so well, he was quite certain Claire had gone in there and not come out.

'You too,' Jeff retorted. 'What in hell

makes you so different, anyways?'

The barkeep shrugged, changed his white coat for a jacket, and then left the saloon. Jeff waited until the remainder of the grumbling men and women had filed outside, then he went across to the main doors and shut them, drawing the bolt. Outside the building in the shadows the barkeep watched what happened, then he glided along the boardwalk, round the side of the big building, and so presently gained the window which he knew belonged to the office. After glancing about him cautiously he tapped gently on the panes.

Nothing happened. His face becoming grim, he tugged out his jack-knife, slipped it between the sashes and snapped back the catch, then raised the lower half of the window gently.

'Anybody in?' he whispered, peering into the gloom.

The sound of a strangled murmur was sufficient for him. He slid over the edge of the sill and came into the office silently, presently reaching Claire's futilely struggling form. The jack-knife blade did the rest and she gasped thankfully as the gag fell away from her mouth.

'It's you, Joey, is it?' she whispered, peering at him in the dim light. 'Thank heaven! This is Jeff's doing.'

'Yeah, so I figgered. I knew you came in — an' when he said you'd gone home I couldn't make it out. I've too much of a likin' for you, miss, to see you knocked around by a skunk like that. You'd best be on your way whilst you're safe . . . So had I, come to think of it. Jeff'll blow me brains out if he finds what I've done. Queer it never dawned on him somebody might release you — or mebbe he figgered nobody would have the nerve. Okay — I'll help you through the window — '

'Not just at this moment,' Claire interrupted. 'I want to find out what Jeff is doing — if I can. What's going on in the saloon? How come you managed to get away to come and rescue me?'

'Jeff turned everybody out of the

saloon — me included, which wasn't such a smart move on his part, come to think of it.'

'Everybody? You mean — he's gone too, with those men who go around with him?'

'I dunno. Possible they're still there. I got the idea Jeff was goin' to hold some kind of conference an' didn't want any outsiders in on it.'

Claire moved silently across the room to the office door. From behind it there came a low murmur of voices, quite inaudible as far as making sense was concerned.

'The table — the little one,' she breathed. 'Give me a hand to pull it to the door here. If I stand on it I'll be just able to reach the fanlight and open it.'

'Okay.'

She and Joey moved silently in the dark and to put the table into position, after clearing its top, was only the work of a moment or two. The barkeep helped the girl up on it, then she straightened up and very gently drew aside the catch on the fanlight, opening it imperceptibly outwards. Immediately the voices of the men beyond came floating through quite distinctly. At the moment it was Lefty who was speaking.

'Y'mean that Tanworth's a *marshal?*' he gasped. 'But — but I reckon that ain't possible! Marshals don't go around shootin' folk — an' we know for a fact that Tanworth shot a guy point blank, right in the saloon here.'

'That must ha' been trickery,' Jeff snapped. 'Fact remains I've got the low-down. It was that dame Claire Henderson who told me — an' I'm durned sure she wasn't lyin', not the way *I* beat the truth outa her — anyways, as I was sayin' I've kept my eye on Tanworth ever since I escaped from him this morning. Not thirty minutes ago I saw him ridin' hell fur leather outa town, hittin' the north trail. There's only one place y'can come to, followin' the north trail, and that's Barville. I give yuh one guess what he might be goin' there fur.'

'To put the police wise?' one of the punchers suggested.

'Nothin' else but. That's why I'm here, t'save you all walkin' into a trap, fur you can be pretty sure that that's what he's fixed when he arranged that raid. You'll ride right into the arms of the law, and that'll be that! Only things won't get that fur,' Jeff finished venomously. 'We're goin' right after him an' take care of him afore he c'n do any damage. It's pretty certain that he hasn't told anybody yet, 'cos he wouldn't dare use a telegraph, an' he certainly hasn't ridden outa town until tonight. So, let's be goin' — quick.'

There was a sound of chairs being pushed aside hastily, of murmuring voices, and heavily treading feet. Claire got down quickly from the table and caught hold of Joey in the dark. It did not take her above thirty seconds to explain things to him.

'Say, that's bad,' he muttered. 'If they catch him up — as I guess they will if they ride hard — they'll wipe him out.

153

Only thing I can see for it is to telegraph the authorities, tell 'em what's brewin', and have them ride from the opposite direction to try and save him.'

'Wouldn't be any use,' Claire decided. 'They're too far away. I'm the only one that can save this — I'm going to try and beat those outlaws to it and catch Thorn up in time to warn him. There is a short cut from the northward trail and if I can use it I might get away with it. My pinto's about the fastest horseflesh there is.'

Without wasting any further time on words she hurried to the open window. When she was satisfied there were no signs of gunmen on view outside — they had evidently already started off on their pursuit of Thorn down the trail — she slipped out into the darkness with Joey's help. He dropped beside her.

'What about me? Want any help?' he enquired.

'No, thanks all the same. My horse is

probably faster than the one you've got, and riding solo I can go all out. I've a gun in my hotel room and my horse is stabled there. Thanks for everything, Joey. Keep your fingers crossed for me.'

Claire turned away in the gloom, moved swiftly along the narrow passage at the side of the building, and so gained the ill-lit high street. There was nobody in sight. She went swiftly across it to her hotel, delayed only long enough to change into outdoor riding clothes and get her loaded automatic, then she returned to the stables at the back of the building and quickly saddled her mount.

A few minutes later she was hurtling down the main street as fast as she could go, her heels digging hard into the animal's side, her hands giving the reins full play so the swift little creature could go all out. At top speed she left the main street behind and began a headlong rush along the northward trail under the stars, the fresh keen air from the mountains threshing back the hair from her face. As the animal thundered along gamely she kept a sharp watch ahead of her. Somewhere, about two miles distant, there was a sudden fork. By using it she could cut some five miles off the journey and rejoin the northward trail later on. It was her only chance if she were to reach Thorn ahead of the trigger-men. According to her calculations they would be beyond the fork on the main trail when she branched off, which would make it just possible for her to get ahead of them — and stay ahead of them.

'Faster,' she murmured in the pinto's ear. 'Give it everything you've got!'

The horse, with an added nudge for good measure, understood — and his already tremendous speed increased to a breakneck gallop. The girl full well knew that he could not keep it up. The essential thing was to get ahead of the trigger-men; only then might it be possible to ease off the frantic pace.

Then, suddenly, as she neared the fork she beheld dim figures looming ahead of her. Startled she tried to draw the pinto to a halt, but it was too late for that. By the time the animal had slowed his headlong pace Claire found herself blundering into the midst of the shadowy figures in the starlight. Before she could get at her gun, or do a thing to save herself, she was dragged from the saddle and flung down on the ground.

Dazed, she was hauled to her feet. The outlines of broad shoulders and Stetson hats were visible against the stars, but the kerchief masks made faces unrecognizable. Until the unmistakable voice of Jeff spoke.

'Well, I don't know how you managed to get away, sister — an' I don't care. It certainly ain't goin' to do you much good ... What were you figgerin' on doin'? Warnin' your boy-friend?'

'Of course I was!' Claire blazed, sheer frustration and fury making her regardless of her words. 'I heard all you planned to do when you were in the saloon. I escaped from those ropes — '

'You couldn't've. Somebody did it for you,' Jeff snapped. 'Who was it?' Then as Claire didn't answer he struck her savagely across the face with the flat of his hand. 'I said who *was* it?' he yelled.

'I should tell you!' Claire retorted defiantly.

'If anybody I reckon it'd be the barkeep,' Lefty's voice said — and the second shadowy figure became identified. 'I noticed he was lookin' mighty suspiciously towards that office door. Ain't done him much good anyways.'

'Do him less when I catch up on him,' Jeff muttered. 'I'll shoot his liver out for this. An' you take us for mugs?' he barked at the girl. 'What did y'think we wus goin' to do? Follow your boyfriend all the way to Barville? We ain't that crazy, kid! Some of the boys have gone ahead: others have spread out — an' Lefty an' me are stayin' here at this trail fork. That means that when your boyfriend comes back — as he'll have to, we'll get him — no matter which way he comes. Be sorta interes- tin' fur you, I reckon, seein' your boyfriend ridin' straight into the trap an' not bein' able to do anythin' about it. I guess this'll be as good a time as any to take care of th' both of you. He deserves all he gets does Tanworth . . . goin' to lead *us* into a trap, was he? He's due for a shock. An' by the time the authorities get here we'll be on our way and you and Tanworth won't count fer much in this world.'

In the face of these impossible circumstances Claire could find noth- ing to say. She was forced down into the grass between the two men, so that none of them were visible against the skyline. The horses were moved into the ditch bordering the trail, and there tethered. Not a sound disturbed the night, save for the distant sounds of a mountain lion ever and again. As she lay there beneath the stars Claire struggled desperately to think of some plan, some ingenious strategy, to take the two triggermen off their guard and warn Thorn in time . . . but no action presented itself.

It was perhaps an hour later when Jeff uttered a cold warning.

'If you try anythin' when Tanworth comes in sight you'll get a bullet pronto — an' don't ferget it. He'll come this far 'cos the rest of the boys have orders from me to let him through but to keep track of him in case anythin' should go wrong an' we happen to miss him. Only thing that *can* go wrong is you tryin' somethin' funny, I reckon. Well, a rod'll take care of that.'

'There's a better way,' Lefty said. 'Gag her. She can't do nothin' then in the way of screamin'. I shouldn't be so handy with your hardware if I were you, Jeff.'

'Oh, you wouldn't, huh? An' who in hell are you to tell me what to do?'

'I'm not tellin' you anythin'; but the gal ain't as tough a customer to handle as a man. No reason why y'should haveta waste bullets on her.'

'Getting' soft, that's what,' Jeff

decided. 'Keep your trap shut from here on, Lefty, an' leave me to handle things as I see best.'

Lefty said no more, and Claire did not speak at all even though she was inwardly grateful for the effort the trigger-man had made to try and save her from Jeff. Then, in the gloom, Jeff's hands were near her face and a kerchief was pulled tight between her teeth and knotted at the back of her head.

'No tellin' when your boyfriend'll be back,' Jeff explained. 'I'm not takin' any chances.'

With that he pushed Claire down again in the grass, and the long, wearying vigil through the night hours continued. How long a time passed Claire had no idea, but as nothing transpired she began to be filled with the wild hope that perhaps Thorn had somehow smelled trouble and taken steps to circumvent it — perhaps even returned to Twin Pines by some roundabout route and — Claire shook her head to herself. This was pure wishful thinking. There was *no* other way into Twin Pines from Barville except this one.

'Wonder how much longer the jigger's goin' to be?' Lefty muttered. 'I'm getting' cramp stuck here in this grass. If he don't get a move on it'll be dawn and we shan't be able to do much for fear of bein' seen.'

'I know that as much as you do,' Jeff retorted nastily. 'He'll be along soon. What's that?' He broke off sharply, and Claire could see his hand raised intently against the stars.

It sounded like the far distant cry of a night bird. After a moment or two it was repeated.

'It's Al,' Lefty breathed tensely. 'The signal. Tanworth's on his way. Al must ha' spotted him.'

'Yeah . . . ' There was grim satisfaction in Jeff's voice. 'This is th' moment I've been waitin' fur — '

He tugged his gun from its holster and Claire waited in taut suspense, every nerve strained as she listened. It

seemed eternities before anything happened, then faintly out of the night
there came the sound of speeding hoofs
along the trail, the queer, drum-like
reverberation becoming louder with
every moment.

'He's nearly here,' Jeff said curtly.
'You watch the girl; I'll fix him.'

He half stood up and waited, then as
the figure of a horseman became visible
against the stars Jeff fired twice into the
air and shouted simultaneously.

'Get off your horse, Tanworth. You're
covered! One wrong move and the girl
gets it. She's in the ditch beside me.'

Thorn dragged his horse to a jolting
halt and was silhouetted for a moment
as a pitching figure with hands raised.
Then he slid down from the saddle to
the trail. He had hardly done so before
there was the sound of more hoofs and
gradually the rest of the party came up.
Surrounded by a score of men Thorn
could do nothing. His expression was
invisible but his voice was grim.

'Seems I underestimated you, Jeff. I

shouldn't have taken chances with a snake, I guess.'

'You ain't so smart, Marshal,' Jeff agreed bitterly. 'Okay, Lefty, let him see the gal in case he don't believe it.'

Claire found her arm seized, and she was forced up the bank from the ditch.

'Ungag her,' Jeff ordered curtly. 'I reckon it doesn't matter now if she screams her head off.'

The kerchief was wrenched away and for a moment or two the girl drew in deep breaths of the night air gratefully. Then she spoke.

'Sorry, Thorn. There was nothing I could do. I rode out to try and warn you but I ran into these cut-throats instead.'

'Whatever it was I'm sure you did your best,' he said quietly; then, his voice becoming ominous, he added, 'Well, what do you skunks plan to do? Won't do you any good, you know. The authorities know everything now and if anything happens to me, or Miss Henderson, you'll be smoked out for the low-down collection of rats you are.'

'Won't matter much since we won't be around,' Jeff commented sourly. 'We got sense enough to keep one jump ahead of th' authorities — don't you forget it. What they do doesn't matter. What *does* matter is that we're goin' t' take care o' you and this gal now — tonight — right now! There's goin' to be a neck-tie party.'

'Why the girl?' Thorn demanded bitterly. 'It's me you hate because I'm a marshal an' out to get you — '

'An' the gal's done her level best to help you!' Jeff broke in. 'Think we're goin' to stand fer that? Not on your life! I was goin' to enjoy myself with her later on but this sorta changes my plans. She's dangerous — an' she's goin' t'hang, same as you are. Tie his hands, boys, and shove him back on his horse. Do the same to the gal — an' be quick about it. Dawn ain't so far away.'

Thorn and the girl both remained passive as their wrists were lashed firmly behind them, then they were lifted to their respective mounts and made to move forward. The journey the trigger-men took led away from the trail — under Jeff's directions — and across pasture land. It ended at an outcropping of cedar trees, all of them with low, strong branches, perhaps half a mile distant.

'Okay — this'll do,' Jeff said curtly. 'Leave them on their horses and get the ropes ready. The boyfriend first. Might as well give the gal a treat.'

There was a low chuckle of amusement from some of the men as they dismounted. Then Claire's voice broke into the quiet.

'Thorn, for God's sake, there must be *something* you can do! Don't you realize what we — ?'

'I realize it,' he interrupted, his voice grim. 'An' I also know when I'm licked.'

It seemed such an abject admission of defeat the girl did not say any more. She watched in horrified silence in the dim light as a lariat was thrown over the branch of the tree near them, the noosed end of the rope being fastened about Thorn's neck. He remained motionless — until the two men holding the rope had moved to the back of the horse on which he was mounted. Then he stooped forward slightly and muttered something in the animal's ear —

Instantly things happened!

The animal, clearly of the spirited type and sensitive to Thorn's every word, suddenly lashed out with both its back feet in the style of a newly-saddled bronco. The flying hoofs struck one man in the face and he went down with a smashed nose. The other got the iron hoof under his jaw and went flying backwards to land knocked out. The two happenings only occupied perhaps three seconds, and the rope the men had been holding was swinging free.

'On your way!' Thorn breathed, digging his knees into the saddle and spurring the creature gently — and immediately the horse hurtled forward into the gloom, gathering speed and giving Thorn an anxious few minutes as he struggled to remain in the saddle. Then, gradually, he worked his bound hands backwards until he was gripping the well-packed saddle-bag. This gave him support — and something else. His fingers began tugging away the strap from the buckle as the uncontrolled horse hurtled on through the night. Despite the distance it had already travelled — for Thorn had changed mounts at Barville and taken over this sorrel of which he was particularly fond — it was refreshed from the brief rest and ready for action.

Back at the site of the cedar trees events had happened so swiftly Jeff and his cohorts had no time to comprehend anything. The instant they did so three of the men dived for their mounts, swung on to them, and began a desperate chase in the direction Thorn had taken.

Thorn, as he struggled with the saddle-bags, could hear the distant thunder of hoofs in pursuit and it gave him added urgency. In the saddle-bag were provisions, a knife, rope, and two spare loaded guns. Without such 'emergency equipment' no man was safe making a trip across the desert and back. At the moment the knife was his main object, and by degrees — as swiftly as the jolting of the sorrel would permit — he dragged the weapon out, working the blade across the ropes binding his hands. The moment he had them free the rest was easy. He straightened up, pushed the knife in his belt and looked behind him. Extra guns he did not need. His own had not been removed, so sure had Jeff been of his ground.

Staring into the starlit dark he could see no signs of his pursuers even though he could hear them not so very far away. He smiled to himself and then forced his horse onwards. He was now following the recognizable trail and if he remembered rightly there were two tall spurs of rock perched on either side of it not so very far ahead.

He was right. In another five minutes he had reached them. Dismounting swiftly he tugged a lariat from his saddle-bag, jumped to the ground, and swiftly fastened the lariat low down on the left-hand rock, carrying it across to the right-hand one so that it spanned the trail. Then he drew his horse to cover and waited.

Presently the dim reverberation of hoofs became noticeable again, growing ever louder. It was not very long before the three men in pursuit of him became visible, moving at breakneck speed — until the horses reached the rope drawn taut across the trail; then the effort was cataclysmic. All three horses stumbled and fell, hurling their riders into the dust.

Instantly Thorn sprang into action. He slapped each horse viciously on the withers as it staggered up and sent all three tearing off in blind panic into the wilderness. Then he whirled back to the saddle of his own mount and was racing away into the dark as futile shots followed him.

'Those gents are going to have a nice long walk back, feller,' he murmured to his horse. 'Now move fast as you can, back to where we came from.'

The animal understood and, if anything, moved faster than ever, hurtling back down the trail, then branching off it in the direction of the cedar tree clump where Claire had been left. As he travelled, desperately afraid that he might be too late to save the girl, Thorn tugged his knife from his belt and held it ready. He planned swift, irresistible strategy: nothing else would suffice, and as far as he was concerned there would be no time for gunplay.

The outlaws, he noticed, were still there as he came hurtling up across the pasture land. The dim light of coming dawn revealed them clearly — and he also saw that Claire was there too, astride her pinto, hands behind her and a rope thrown about the tree branch and noosed about her neck.

Revolvers exploded. Thorn ignored them because he could do nothing else. Regardless of everything he raced his sorrel through the midst of the men and reached out with his knife blade at the same moment. It slashed through the rope about the girl's neck and instantly he dropped his arm, clutching her round the waist. She was swept backwards in his grip, followed by an explosion of revolver shots and the curses of men who had been kicked or trampled in the rush.

Then Thorn was gone, hauling the girl into the saddle in front of him, forcing the snorting horse onward at a pace which must have strained it to the uttermost. But it did not give in. It kept on going with a dogged, determined run.

'Only just made it,' Thorn panted, holding the girl tightly.

'Only just is right,' she breathed. 'Another five seconds and they'd have kicked my horse from under me and left me swinging. In fact they'd have done it some time before that only there was an argument. Lefty did his best to save me: in fact, he'd tried all along — but Jeff wouldn't have it. Result was Lefty got a bullet.'

'He did, huh? One less to bother about . . . More I see of Jeff the more of a snake I think he is. And, by the way, those two men who were working for me — the one I was supposed to 'shoot' and the chap who helped him — were bumped off. Must have been Black Yankee's doing. I heard about it at headquarters — '

Thorn broke off and glanced behind him sharply at the noise of hurtling hoofs. Quickly he turned the sorrel's head and bore sharp left, thereafter continuing an evading movement which led ever nearer to the mountains, grey in the approaching dawn. After some ten minutes of breakneck riding he began to slow the panting animal down.

'Okay,' he murmured. 'I reckon we've

given them the slip all right by now.'

'And what comes next?' the girl asked.

'Best thing we can do is go into the mountains. We'll be safe there, and there are caves where we can shelter. I've a good supply of food and drink in my saddle-bag, so we shan't starve. Once there we'll have to think out what we do next. This has thrown all the plans I had into utter confusion.'

Claire nodded but did not say anything. Reducing the horse's progress to a jog trot Thorn kept on going, presently following an upwardly rising trail from the pasture land which led into an ever rockier region. Gradually, as the ascent continued, the daylight waxed, and by the time a huge natural cave had been gained in the higher foothills the first shafts of the newly risen sun were blasting down from a cobalt blue sky.

'This'll do,' Thorn decided, dismounting. 'We've a good view of anything from here too. That'll help us to take care of anybody who tries to follow.'

He held up his hands and lifted the girl down beside him, then he led the tired horse into the shade of the rocks, unpacked some meal for him from the saddle-bag, and filled a tin container with water. This done, he turned, took the girl's arm, and led the way into the cave. It was large, dry and airy — as well as being a complete protection from the torrid Arizona sunlight.

'Time we had a meal an' a rest too,' Thorn decided. 'Make yourself comfortable, Claire, whilst I see what I can rustle up for us . . . '

9

It was also just after dawn when Jeff and his men straggled back into Twin Pines, their mounts loping through the empty high street. At this hour the denizens of the cock-eyed town were not yet astir.

In the centre of the street, only a few yards from Ma Brendick's rooming house, Jeff drew to a halt — and the rest of his cohorts did likewise. He looked grimly round upon them. Of the original twenty, three were missing. The two men who had been kicked by Thorn's horse had died from their injuries, and Lefty had been taken care of by Jeff's own gun. The three who had been thrown from their horses were mounted double saddle with three other men, nor were they looking particularly energetic after the long, gruelling walk they had had back to

176

the cedar tree site.

'Well, Jeff, what's next?' asked Al, with a bitter glance. 'If you ask me our best move is to get movin' quick. Now that marshal's gotten away with everything — the gal included — it doesn't look too mighty healthy fer us, does it?'

'The whole scheme was crazy,' another remarked sourly. 'We should have stopped him *before* he had the chance to go to the authorities — not waited fer him comin' back. Now the authorities know all about it and they'll be down after us like a pack of coyotes afore we know where we are.'

'You guys can run if you like,' Jeff snapped. 'I'm stayin' right here. Fur one thing there's plenty to be picked up on the ranches around here — once the heat of the chase has died down — an' fur another I'm willin' to bet Tanworth'll come back into town yet. Don't see how he can avoid it. When he does I'll be ready for him. I'll drill him neat — an' that girl too if I can get near enough. He may think he was mighty smart last night but I can be smart too if need be.'

'It's needless risk!' Al protested. 'Yore behavin' plain crazy, Jeff. Tanworth's a marshal with all the weight o' the law behind him. He'll spring something an' get you — and the rest of us.'

'Supposin' he does?' Jeff asked sourly. 'We got guns, ain't we? 'Sides, I don't think the law *will* come right into town. The scheme, as I think Tanworth figgered it, was for us to make that raid on the Double-S tonight an' so run into the law. Naturally, we won't do that. What we *must* do is guard all the trails leadin' to Barville an' make sure Tanworth doesn't try an' get to headquarters to tell 'em the plans are changed. If we can prevent that it means the rangers'll turn up at the ranch to nab us — they thinkin' everything's all set. But what's to happen if we nab them instead?'

The trigger-men started and then glanced at each other.

'Simple enough, ain't it?' Jeff said

grimly. 'An ambush! I reckon there won't be more'n a dozen rangers after us — if that. If we're there first we can pick 'em off one by one. That'll teach 'em to poke their noses in.'

'Yeah,' Al said slowly, 'that's all right — but there's another side to it. Don't y'think yore kinda lettin' things get outa hand, Jeff? That sort of thing, wipin' out members of the law, can start the biggest man-hunt goin', an' we'd be in the middle of it. Not so sure I like th' thought o' that.'

'Speak for yourselves,' Jeff responded, shrugging. 'I'm a wanted man anyways — doesn't count to me how many folk I kill so long as I keep livin'. I've only one neck to stretch when they *do* catch up on me. I'm aimin' to make this territory so hot for the law that they'll leave us alone. If those guys ride out to get us, and not one of 'em goes back, they'll think twice back at Barville headquarters.'

'Else they'll dig out every man they've got an' come here an' give us hell,' Al commented gloomily.

Jeff made an impatient movement. 'It's up to you guys. Think it over — have a sleep — an' then meet me in the Lucky Horseshoe this evenin'. If yore willin' we can take care of these pals of Tanworth's. If yore not — well, mebbe I'll go gunnin' fer them on my own. They're my born enemies, remember, an' I don't care what lengths I go to to make 'em sit up.'

'An' what about Tanworth?' one of the men questioned. 'An' the gal too, if it comes t' that? They go free?'

Jeff shook his head. 'Only one place where they c'n hide, an' that's the mountain foothills. Mebbe they've got some food and drink to carry on with fur a while, but it won't last forever. In the end they'll have to break cover — an' when they do it'll be just too bad fur them. One of you is goin' to keep a watch on those foothills. The only place they can come for more food an' drink is right here in Twin Pines.'

'I don't envy the guy who's goin' to

keep on the watch for 'em,' Al remarked.

''Bout time you did, then,' Jeff told him sourly. 'Yore goin' to be the guy.'

* * *

After they had had a breakfast of sorts, Thorn and the girl took it in turns to get some sleep; then towards midday they were both refreshed and more in trim for considering the position in which they found themselves. Together they sat in the cave entrance, looking out from their high eyrie over the foothills and beyond them again to the pasture land. Remote, far away, like a toy town, Twin Pines was visible in the glare of the noonday sun.

'Well? Any plans?' Claire asked at length.

For a little while Thorn did not answer. He continued smoking the cigarette he had rolled for himself, gazing out over the endless shimmering expanse.

'I've been doing plenty of thinking, anyway,' he said finally. 'To get some angle on this, Claire, I have to try and figger what *Jeff* will do, and then do my best to make things fit accordingly. He's not the kind of man to take defeat lying down — so that leaves him two courses open. Either he'll come in this direction gunning for you and me — or else he'll wait until we have to break cover through lack of food and drink. And on the other hand he'll have guessed by what the rest of the boys have told him that the Double-S raid was nothing else but a trap.'

'And how far does that get us?'

'He may try and attack the men who'll be at the Double-S tonight waiting to arrest the gang.'

'Tackle the rangers, you mean?' Claire gazed in astonishment. 'He wouldn't be such an idiot, surely?'

'I think he would,' Thorn decided grimly. 'Jeff's no fool. Since he must know the raid was a trap, he must also know that men will be there to make an arrest. And they'll ride straight into a hail of lead unless I can think of some way to stop it.'

Claire said nothing immediately. It had never occurred to her that Jeff might go to such lengths. She had had the notion that once realizing he had lost the round he would hit the trail and never come back.

'Jeff an' his boys are in a pretty strong position,' Thorn resumed, after a while. 'He's the undisputed boss now; no doubt of that. And there isn't even Lefty around to put something of a brake on things. Twin Pines is a pretty unique stronghold in many ways. It has only one entrance — from the north — from which direction any invaders — rangers for instance — are bound to come. And they could be picked off like flies by Jeff and his boys if they were so minded. The other end of the town runs into desert, remember . . . '

Thorn's voice trailed off and he sat gazing fixedly into distances. The girl looked at him curiously.

'Anything wrong?'

'Er — no,' he replied, jerking himself back to awareness. 'Sorry, a thought just got me. About the town having only one end, I mean. Gettin' back to cases, Jeff has no need to run for it. If he acts smart he can hold out indefinitely in Twin Pines, and I don't think he'd have much difficulty, aided by those who are now workin' beside him, in forcing the rest of the populace to do his bidding if it came to it. Which means Twin Pines has become a genuine outlaw's town instead of a half-hearted one.'

'None of which,' Claire said, 'clears up the problem of how you are going to warn the rangers of the dangers they'll run into tonight. Only solution is for you to either telegraph them or ride to Barville and tell them — isn't it?'

'If it were that simple I wouldn't be sitting here. I can't do either of these things. The trail to Barville will be watched and the telegraph is right out. I've no other course,' Thorn finished,

'but to let things take their course —
but at nightfall I'll see what I can do to
intercept the boys and give 'em the
tip-off.'

'And I'm included, of course?' the
girl asked. 'You don't expect me to stay
here all alone biting my fingerends, do
you?'

''Course not.' Thorn smiled and
patted her arm.

'Well, then, that's the plan for now.
For the rest of the day we'd better keep
our eyes skinned and see what happens.'

But nothing did. Throughout all the
hours of daylight they were constantly
on the alert for any sign of horsemen
approaching, a fact which would have
been heralded by the inevitable feathers
of dust stirred by a horse's hoofs and
visible for miles — but the foothills and
pasture land remained undisturbed.
Several times Thorn cursed the fact that
he had no field-glasses with him. With
the comings and goings of the people of
Twin Pines visible, but not so visible as

185

to be distinct, it was exasperating not to be able to properly determine what was going on.

'Incidentally,' the girl said, when they had completed an evening meal together, 'which *is* the Double-S? There seem to be dozens of spreads scattered around the landscape down there.'

Thorn pointed northwards to an extensive ranch with big corrals to one side of it. It was easily distinguishable for its size.

'That's it — and the annoying part is that to reach it from here there's little or no rock cover — just a straight run down through the foothills and across the pasture land. If we attempted a ride like that by daylight we'd be sittin' pigeons for any trigger-men Jeff may have lyin' round waiting.'

Claire nodded, sighed, and leaned back comfortably against the rocks. The hardest task from now on was to kill time — but it had to be done. Hardly exchanging any words she and Thorn watched the shadows lengthen across the wilderness below, saw the sun begin to dip in a flood of gold and vermilion, and at last there came the distant purple mists that heralded the coming of the twilight.

Once it started it gathered impetus rapidly and the day gave place to night with hardly any noticeable intermission. Cool, refreshing wind began to blow down the mountain heights.

'Okay,' Thorn murmured, stirring, and holding down his hand to the girl against the stars. 'I think we can start movin' now.'

'Wish I had my pinto,' she said in regret, standing beside him. 'He was a grand little horse.'

'Since you haven't you'll ride beside me. Maybe all the better; we're not so likely to lose touch.'

Thorn turned into the back of the cave, saddled the horse, and then brought it out into the open. He lifted the girl up to the saddle and then swung into position before her. Gently he urged the sorrel forward and, sheer-footed animal that he was, he picked his way amidst the loose stones, going gradually ever downwards along the declivity. As they neared the base of the foothills Thorn rode more cautiously in an effort to prevent the animal making any noise with its hoofs.

'Seems quiet enough,' the girl murmured, looking about her. 'And it won't be moonrise for long enough.'

'Which is all to the good,' Thorn commented. 'Best thing we can do is head northwards and try and intercept the boys as they ride in.'

He put this plan into action, keeping well clear of the vicinity of the Double-S ranch in the distance. By a wide detour he gradually began to approach the point where the trail itself began. Then, as he was passing a particularly dense manzanita thicket, there came a sudden report from a gun.

Instantly Thorn drew rein and swung round in the saddle, his revolver in his hand. Before he had the chance to fire there was a second arrow of flame from the thicket, the whang of a bullet, then Thorn felt as if the universe exploded in his skull. He reeled out of the saddle and dropped with a heavy impact into the dust.

'Thorn!' Claire screamed hoarsely, jumping down beside him and clutching at his shoulders. '*Thorn!*'

He failed to move despite all her struggles, then she looked up and around at the sound of hurrying feet. Some half-dozen men came up in the starlight and dragged her to a standing position again.

'Well, thanks for comin' past just at this point,' Jeff's voice remarked. 'Couldn't ha' bin better if you'd arranged it. We weren't lookin' fer you; just chance — an' a lucky shot.'

'You've shot Thorn!' the girl shouted desperately. 'Killed him maybe. You dirty, low-down killer you — '

'Shut up!' The outlaw's hand impacted violently across her face and she recoiled; then he turned to the fallen man and kicked him casually.

'Lucky shot that, Jeff,' Al commented. 'In this light.'

'Lucky or otherwise it got him . . . '

Jeff went down on his knees and made a closer examination. When he straightened up again his tone was grimly satisfied.

'Got him in the head. I reckon we can leave him here. He's bleeding pretty freely and with no one to help him he'll pass out nice and peaceful like. Can't afford any more slugs. Need 'em for all the rangers when they turn up. All right you,' Jeff barked to the girl, his fingers sinking crushingly into her arm. 'Yore comin' with us. This way!'

Tugging and straining she was forced along the rough ground, compelled to leave Thorn where he was and watch his horse sent galloping madly into the distance as it received a violent slap across the withers.

'Down there, you — in the thicket,' Jeff ordered, and Claire was flung on her face amidst the gorse-like branches of the stuff, an iron grip still pinning her wrist.

'Once we get tonight over,' Jeff told her after a while, as the men formed in a watchful group to the rear, 'then mebbe you an' me can have that good time we planned together, huh?'

Claire did not answer. She was too terrified, too appalled at the thought of Thorn lying out there, dying from loss of blood.

'Say — I hear somethin',' the voice of Al said abruptly. 'Like riders in the distance — listen!'

He was right. Claire's quick ears picked up the sound too when it was far away. Gradually it came nearer, the hoof beats of perhaps a dozen horse-men.

'Yeah, it's them,' Jeff muttered, and there was the click of his revolver hammer drawing back. 'They'll not be ten yards from us when they pass this point. You boys got your guns ready?'

'Sure!'

'You bet!'

'Okay, you know what to do — which just gives me time for this — '

Jeff whipped off his kerchief and bound it tightly round Claire's mouth, then he pushed her flat on the ground and put one knee in the small of her back so he could be sure where she was when his attention was otherwise engaged. Smothered, hardly able to breathe, she lay waiting — until hell itself broke loose.

The hoof beats of the approaching riders had come distinctly upon her senses when the noise of them was drowned by the explosion of guns around her. Immediately the riders fired back and dust and chippings of the thicket flew into the girl's face as she lay panting and struggling with Jeff firing his guns relentlessly.

So great was the confusion and noise Claire had not the least idea how the battle went. Once or twice she found herself in danger of being trampled on as a horse and rider galloped near the thicket — then the immediate peril receded again. The exchange of bullets seemed to last several minutes, dying down presently into single shots followed by an ominous quiet broken only by the whinnying of frightened horses.

'All right, that's enough,' Jeff ordered curtly, holstering his guns. 'We did it — just as we figgered. Took care of every one of 'em. Wouldn't ha' done if Tanworth had had his way, I reckon.'

Slowly the crouching men rose up against the stars. Claire found the gag pulled roughly from her mouth and Jeff returned it to his neck.

'How far do you suppose this mass killing will ever get you?' she demanded desperately. 'Nearly a dozen rangers wiped out. The law will never rest now until it's got you strung up — which is more than you deserve, any of you! 'Specially you men who were decent citizens of Twin Pines until this skunk, and Black Yankee, and the others came into town.'

'I've warned you once about keepin' your mouth shut,' Jeff said ominously.

'Best heed it or I'll make you smart.'

'What do we do with these guys we've bumped off?' Al asked, looking at the shadowy figures sprawled on the ground in the starlight. 'No guarantee they're all dead.'

'Have to risk that,' Jeff replied. 'No bullets left. Leave 'em where they are. It'll serve as a warnin' to any other jiggers who start gettin' bright ideas — '

'One thing we should take care of,' Al interrupted. 'Like as not Tanworth tipped 'em off at the Double-S about the 'raid' he'd planned. They'll be wonderin' what's gone wrong when it doesn't happen. Mebbe they even heard the shots explodin' . . . fact remains some of 'em may come here and revive these guys that aren't dead, Tanworth among them. What then? I'm not much worried about what these police boys can do — but I am leery of Tanworth. He's a smart guy, an' he'll be fightin' mad if he ever recovers from this night's work.'

'Yeah . . . that's a thought,' Jeff admitted. 'He's the one we've got to be careful of; the rest don't matter. Okay, I guess there's one way to settle it since I've no bullets to make sure of him.'

He got up quickly and strode through the starlight to where he had left Thorn lying. The other men remained near the thicket, waiting, holding the girl tightly. For some time Jeff seemed to be floundering about in the dark — then he came hurrying back at a pace that showed he was anxious about something.

'The jigger's gone!' he ejaculated.

'Gone?' Al repeated stupidly. 'But — but he couldn't've. He got a slug in the head, didn't he — '

'Yeah, but he's gone, I tell you! I don't know when, or how. He can't have gotten far. Better help me search, you boys. Al, you stay with the girl.'

Claire did not laugh outright, though she felt uncommonly inclined to do so. Chiefly it was puzzlement which prevented her. From the appearance of Thorn's head injury he had been knocked out completely, and yet now . . .

She remained passive, Al's gun trained upon her, whilst Jeff and the remainder of the men started off into the starlight. They were gone perhaps ten minutes and returned muttering amongst themselves. Jeff was plainly boiling over with fury.

'No dice?' Al questioned.

'What the hell do you think?' Jeff snarled at him. 'The guy's vanished as completely as though he wus never there. I don't understand it — an' I don't like it neither.'

He stood thinking for a moment or two, then made up his mind.

'He's gone, an' there ain't nothin' we can do about it right now,' he said. 'We'd best hop back into town and take the gal with us. Come on . . . '

10

It was still some time before dawn when the party arrived back in Twin Pines' main street. Jeff lowered Claire from the saddle where he had been holding her, and then dropped down beside her.

'I reckon there's one place where you'll be safe,' he told her. 'Safe, I mean, from tryin' to escape an' makin' more trouble. An' that's the jail. Now Tanworth's missin' I'm callin' myself sheriff — so that gives me the jail to use if I want.'

'What good do you suppose it will do locking me up in jail?' Claire snapped.

'As fur as Tanworth's concerned it'll do all the good in the world. If he's able to make any attempt to find you — an' I reckon he will — there's one place where he can't break into, an' that's the jail.'

He did not waste any further time on

words. Still gripping her arm tightly he forced her along the street, up the three steps which led to the boardwalk, and so to the sheriff's office. The outer door was locked but three savage kicks soon broke it open. Stumblingly, Claire was forced through the small outer office and then to the single cell at the rear of the place. In the dim light she could not see Jeff, but she heard the clang as he slammed the door upon her, and then the rasp of the key.

Satisfied, he returned to the starlit gloom of the main street and considered the shadowy figures of the men.

'Well, you mugs, what are yuh goin' to do?' he asked briefly. 'Run out, or stick around?'

'There wouldn't be much sense in runnin' out now,' Al observed. 'The entire law'll be after us after what we've done. Nothin' fur it but to stay an' shoot it out if need be. Part I don't like is Tanworth bein' missin'. I'd give anythin' to know what that guy's up to.'

'Yeah,' Jeff mused, staring into the gloomy distances. 'Yeah — so would I.'

★ ★ ★

At this moment Thorn was lying beside a water hole about a mile from the Double-S ranch. It was still dark and he half lay as he dabbed at himself with his sodden kerchief. Near him, nibbling at sparse roots, stood his horse. When he had whistled it it had come to him immediately from the distance where panic at the sound of firing had driven it.

Thorn was not dead, nor anything approaching it. The shot which had hit him had laid an ugly gash across the top of his head, causing a great deal of blood loss — but nothing more. He had recovered consciousness during the firing but, too dazed to be of much help to his fellow officers of the law, he had instead taken advantage of the confusion to creep away to this water hole which he knew lay a little to the south of the Double-S. Now he lay meditating, his strength returning, his face grim.

'Nothin' for it, feller, but to let Jeff and his boys remain in ignorance of what's happened to me,' he murmured to his horse, as the animal drifted towards him. 'Mebbe they'll have looked for me now the shooting's over — mebbe not. Fact remains they don't know where I am or what I'm doing . . . '

He became silent and lay motionless as footfalls sounded not very far away in the still night air. Voices drifted to him on the quiet.

'Not one guy left out of the dozen, Pete. It's bad goin' no matter how y'look at it.'

'Yeah. Can't think what could've gone wrong. No sign of Tanworth neither. Those trigger-men must have gotten wise somehow an' acted fust. Best thing we can do is let the authorities in Barville know what's happened. I'll ride over there in the mornin' and tell 'em. Sooner they send down enough men to clean up this mob an' the better — '

The voices faded as the two men passed out of earshot. Thorn sat up a little. They had been Pete, foreman of the Double-S ranch, and the ranch-owner himself. Evidently they had been investigating the scene of the firing.

'Not one left out of a dozen,' Thorn breathed, clenching his fist. 'That about does it! There's got to be no quarter for Jeff an' his boys. They've got to be hounded out and strung up for this night's work — but the last thing that must happen is for more men to come here and walk right into another massacre. You and me have got to get to Barville, pal, whilst we can,' he added to the horse. 'Now's the time t'do it, too. Ten to one that Jeff an' his boys won't be guardin' the way at this time.'

Thorn got to his feet, tied the damp kerchief round his wounded head, and then climbed into the saddle. He felt unsteady for a moment or two, and then it passed.

'On your way, feller,' he whispered. 'We've got to get as far away from this region as we can before sun-up.'

The horse, which had had more or less a whole day of rest and very little exercise since, galloped forward quickly, Thorn clinging to the saddle horn as dizziness again assailed him. Then the cold, refreshing wind blowing across from the mountains revived him somewhat and he felt stronger.

He got clear of the immediate vicinity of Twin Pines long before dawn. By the time the day had fully come he was feeling himself again. He could even have felt happy but for two things — the gnawing worry of what might be happening to Claire in the ruthless hands of Jeff; and the thought of how much he might yet have to do to bring that sadistic outlaw to justice.

Three times in the long journey to Barville he broke his journey at water-holes, resting the horse and using up what provisions he had left in the saddle-bag. It was towards two o'clock when he entered Barville's main street in the blaze of the sun. He looked, and felt, grimy and unshaven, the dusty bandage about his head. Curious looks followed him as he rode, finally dismounting outside the law offices in the centre of the busy town. He tethered his mount in the shade and then strode up the steps and into the big building. Captain Billings, head of the department, did not delay a moment in seeing him.

'For Pete's sake, what happened to you, Thorn?' he asked in amazement, jumping up and pulling forth a chair. 'You look as if you've been enjoying yourself.'

'I feel as though I have,' Thorn growled, settling down and feeling painfully at the kerchief. 'I've had a bullet across the skull that needs some attention before I start riding again. Anyways, I had to risk coming here to tip you off. Last night was a total failure. Putting it bluntly, you sent out twelve men to clean things up — and you'll be twelve men short from here on. They're dead, every mother's son of 'em.'

Captain Billings sank down slowly again in his chair and stared.

'You mean that that bunch of owl-hooters killed *every one* of our boys?'

'That's just what I mean . . . ' and Thorn outlined the circumstances. Captain Billings' square face was grim at the end of the story.

'I'll get every man I've got, and from other departments as well, and blast these devils right out of the state,' he declared, banging his fist on the desk. 'I'll ride into Twin Pines myself, for that matter, and — '

'No you won't,' Thorn said quietly.

'Won't?' Billings stared. 'Why the devil not? You goin' scared, Thorn, after all that's happened?'

'You know me better than that, sir. All I'm tryin' to point out is that you riding into Twin Pines with a party of men would suit Jeff fine. In fact that's most likely what he's waiting for. Do that and you'd probably lose the rest of your men. Very soon you'll probably have a rancher over here from the Double-S urging you to do that very thing. Fact remains, you mustn't.'

'You're not seriously suggesting we should let Jeff and his cut-throats get away with it?'

'Anything but — but don't overlook two things, sir. On the one hand he has a hostage in the person of Miss Henderson. Her life might be forfeit in retaliation for you riding into town; and for another thing Twin Pines is the kind of town — one-ended — that you can't get into secretly. At least, not a party of you. Jeff and his boys will guard themselves with their very lives from now on. If you rode into town with your men you'd be picked off as you approached. If you were not then, as I say, Miss Henderson might be used as a lever to make you get out.'

'Mmm,' Captain Billings mused. 'I see what you mean . . . then what's the answer?'

'I've got to play a lone hand, that's all — same as I've been doing all along; but this time I have an advantage because Jeff hasn't the least idea what's happened to me. He doesn't even know whether I'm dead or alive. That gives me a certain freedom . . . I've a rough plan worked out. It's the ranch raid in a different form, by which I should be able to drive these gangsters straight into your arms. It'll be dangerous, and I may even get wiped out doing it, because when the time's ripe I intend to walk into Twin Pines as large as life and make an attempt to formally arrest Jeff on a charge of murder.'

'You're crazy!' Billings declared blankly. 'Dammit man, it's asking for it. He'll blow the daylights out of you.'

'Possibly,' Thorn admitted quietly. 'But if he doesn't — and naturally I'll be on my guard — it's likely that all the men you want, Jeff included, will ride

206

straight out and into your ambush. Listen — this is what I'm planning on doing . . . '

Thorn leaned forward intently across the desk and began to explain carefully. Captain Billings hardly spoke during the process, contenting himself with nodding from time to time. When at last he had the details he rubbed his jaw slowly.

'Well, it's an idea,' he admitted. 'Do you think it'll work?'

'Feasible as anything I can think out — but it depends chiefly on my finding Miss Henderson. That may not be easy. For all I know Jeff may have murdered her by this time — though somehow I don't think so. He'd rather have her alive so he can — as he baldly puts it — have 'fun' with her. You know what that means.'

Billings gave a grim nod. 'I can guess. Where do you think she might be?'

'As to that . . . ' Thorn frowned for a while. 'I've given it quite a bit of thought. Jeff certainly won't have her too much on view in case one or other of the townsfolk tries to help her. Most of them like her — particularly the Lucky Horseshoe's barkeep — and if she were in a spot they'd try and help her. There's one place where they couldn't do that, though — if she were in the town's jail.'

'Uh-huh, that's a possibility,' Billings agreed. 'And if that's right it'll be a mighty tough place for you to get her out of.'

'That's my worry. I'll do it somehow. And if she isn't there I'll find out where she is. Once that's done the rest of the plan ought to work. All you have to do is see that the boys are well concealed on the northward trail and ready for action, after sundown tomorrow night.'

'Okay,' Billings promised. 'I'll see to that. And right now I reckon you'd best be taking a rest and have some attention for that head.'

'You're right,' Thorn agreed wearily. 'I can take until sundown before I set off back. An' have an eye to my horse, will you? I'll need a fresh one for the return journey. That cayuse has done more than its share already.'

★   ★   ★

It was well after midnight when Thorn, refreshed and alert again, his head injury vastly improved by medical attention in Barville, returned to the borders of Twin Pines. He approached by the northward trail because there was no other way — but from the complete lack of action it appeared that, as yet anyway, Jeff had no men on guard. None the less Thorn was not taking any chances.

A mile from the town he branched off the main trail and, rocky and treacherous though the route was, forced his mount round to the rear of the town, thereby avoiding the high street and taking cover from the ramshackle buildings. At the back of the hotel where the girl normally stayed he tethered his horse, vaulted up the veranda roof, and then crept silently to the window of the room she used.

It was partly open and he lifted it gently, peering into the dim interior. There were no sounds, and certainly none of deep breathing from a sleeping person.

'No dice,' Thorn muttered to himself. 'Empty. Mebbe you guessed right about the prison after all.'

He lowered the window back in position and returned to his horse. Leading it instead of mounting it he went along the back of the buildings, parallel with the main street, until he came to the rear of the sheriff's office which automatically brought him to the barred window of the small adobe jail at the back. Mounting his horse again to bring him to the required height, he peered between the window bars. There was somebody in the dim light beyond, apparently stretched on the bunk.

'Claire!' Thorn called softly. 'Claire — that you?' Then he dodged back out of sight in case his guess was wrong.

The figure beyond had evidently not heard him for it did not stir. Thorn dismounted, picked up a pebble, and threw it between the bars as he returned to the saddle. Again he waited, concealed against the wall, then he gave a little sigh of relief at the vision of a dim white face in the starlight striving to see outside.

'Claire!' He caught her hands between the bars. 'Then I guessed right. You *are* in the jail!'

The girl did not respond immediately. The shock of discovering Thorn was alive and well was pretty considerable.

'How? What?' she asked at last, keeping her voice low. 'I'd given you up for lost, Thorn — after the bullet you got in the head.'

'A scratch — looked uglier than it was. What's been happening to you? Jeff put you in here, of course?'

'Of course.'

'Just what I expected. What's he been

doing? Making himself objectionably friendly?'

'Not yet,' the girl said quietly. 'I've only seen him once since he pushed me in here around dawn. He's had food sent in to me. He came and had a look, apparently to make sure I was nicely locked away, and then he went off again. Where to I don't know. He's planning something for me; that goes without saying — and for you too if he ever gets his hands on you. One thing I *do* know; he's planning to stay in town and fight it out if any effort is made to arrest him or his boys. And of course that means the rest of the town will have to support him if they value their lives.'

'Naturally. So — '

'But what happened to *you?*' the girl insisted. 'You haven't told me yet.'

Thorn gave her the details and finished, 'So of course the next move is to get you out of here.'

'How? There's a man on guard in the sheriff's office — with a loaded gun.

And when day comes he'll be relieved by another man. Jeff isn't taking any chances. He knows that I can't escape from this cell by the window, and if I could do it by the door I'd have to go through the office to get outside — so there it is. One man in the office is enough.'

'It might so happen,' Thorn said slowly, 'that you are smart enough to defeat that one gent at his own game. For instance, you've got a belt round your riding skirt, haven't you?'

'Uh-huh. What about it?'

'Just give it to me and I'll do the rest. I dunno what'll happen to your skirt,' Thorn added, with a grin in the darkness.

'Nothing will. It stays up by itself. The belt's only decoration.'

There were movements in the gloom, then Thorn found the belt thrust through the space between the bars. He took it and murmured, 'Okay; that's all you have to worry about at the moment. Go back to your bunk and take it easy. I'll be joining you before you know it.'

The girl started to ask questions but Thorn did not give her the chance to complete them. Dismounting from his horse he led it round the building, tied it to the tie rack at the front, then walked silently up on the boardwalk. He tested the door of the sheriff's outer office and found it locked. He only reflected for a moment and then knocked hard upon it.

There was a sound of movement within and an oil lamp suddenly came into being. A shadow danced in front of the glow on the shade-covered window; then a voice came out into the darkness from behind the closed door.

'Who is it?'

'Jeff,' Thorn retorted curtly, in a passable simulation of the outlaw's petulant tone.

A chain rattled behind the door. It was presumably the only means of securing it since Jeff had smashed the lock earlier in the day. Gently Thorn eased his right gun into his hand and jabbed it straight into the man's stomach as the door opened wide.

'All right, inside!' Thorn ordered. 'And be quick about it!'

Taken completely by surprise the man had to obey. With his hands raised he backed into the office and stood glaring at Thorn in the lamplight.

'So it's you,' he muttered. 'I might ha' guessed it. Jeff warned me t'be on the lookout.'

'Pity you weren't,' Thorn commented dryly. 'I'll tell you what I'm going to do with you, my friend. You're taking a ride out into the desert — on the northward trail — and you're going to stay there, bound, until tomorrow night when some of the boys from Barville will be bound to come across you. You'll have an uncomfortable, thirsty time — sure, but you'll survive. Tough guys like you don't harm much in a day's sun. I'd shoot you right now only as a marshal I can't — 'cept in self-defence; so the only other course to keep you out of the

215

way so you can't tell Jeff what happened is the one I've chosen. An' it's going to look as though the gal did it.'

The trigger-man did not say anything but his lips tightened viciously.

'Move!' Thorn ordered. 'To the cell door.'

The outlaw obeyed, leaving the office and walking down the narrow passage until he came outside the cell door. Claire, aware of what was going on, was dimly visible in the light casting from the oil lamp in the office.

'Drop your guns on the floor,' Thorn snapped. 'And if you try and fire them I'll shoot — self-defence.'

The outlaw paused for a moment, then he drew slowly — to suddenly move at lightning speed and fire. It was only the dark which saved Thorn. The bullets missed, but he was thrown off guard. The next thing he knew a butt end of one of the guns had struck him violently behind the ear, knocking him to his knees.

'No room for gunplay, I reckon,' the

outlaw panted, 'but that don't stop fists — ' and his left lashed out with savage violence. It took Thorn clean on the jaw and hurled him violently against the cell door, jolting him badly and knocking his gun out of his hand.

He forced himself straight again, still retaining in his left hand the belt he had taken from the girl. As the gun-hawk lunged at him again Thorn swung the belt suddenly, intending to loop it round the man's neck and use it as a garrotte — but the darkness prevented him striking accurately. The belt missed its mark and a blow in the stomach doubled Thorn up helplessly, another punch in the face straightening him again. Dazed, utterly winded, he stumbled about blindly in the dark, conscious of the fact that he had lost the belt somewhere.

It was the surprise of discovering that the attack was not followed up that made him turn. The outlaw was struggling hard against the cell door, his neck and head jammed against it, whilst on the other side Claire was pulling with all her strength on the belt, bracing her knee against the bars. Frantically though the gun-hawk struggled he could not dislodge the pressure of the belt on his throat.

'I'll show *him*!' Claire panted, and instead of loosening the pressure she increased it, shutting off the man's final grunts of anguish as he fought for air.

'Lay off!' Thorn shouted, blundering forward. 'You'll kill him, Claire! You — '

'Why shouldn't I?' she demanded. 'He's killed plenty of other folks. You dropped the belt, so I might as well use it . . . '

Her determination to be tough, however, was too much at variance with her natural woman's instinct for her to maintain it. She released the belt suddenly and stood back. The outlaw slid to the floor and remained there motionless.

'I — I couldn't finish it,' Claire whispered. 'Don't know why I shouldn't. My grandmother would have done. She was a true Westerner. I'm getting lily-white, I s'pose.'

'Not altogether,' Thorn said, getting up from his knees. 'This guy's dead — but from the look of things it wasn't the strangling that did it. It was the angle his neck was at against the bars. Seems to be broken . . . '

There was silence for a moment. Then Claire's voice sounded horrified.

'This — makes me a murderess, Thorn!'

'Anything but. Strangling *didn't* kill him, I tell you — more chance than anything else. A neck will soon break at the wrong angle. And anyway you only set about him in self-defence — or at least to save me. I'd intended to use that belt by leaving it here as a sort of blind clue to show how you'd probably overpowered this jigger. We might as well leave it round his neck and do the thing properly. The essential thing is for Jeff to think that *you* did everything. I don't want him to know I'm around. Now, let's see if this guy has any keys on him. He should've.'

They were not on the outlaw, but they were in the office, and in a few moments Thorn had the cell door open, leaving the keys dangling in the lock.

'This will be a nice little set-up for Jeff to figger out when he comes across it,' he murmured, taking the girl's arm. 'Now let's get out of here before anything else happens.'

'To where? There's no place in town that will be safe from Jeff or his boys.'

'We're going to our cave in the mountain foothills. That's one place Jeff and his boys can never reach without us seeing them first. He won't follow. Unless I miss my guess he'll think you've managed to escape by killing your jailer and may be just anywheres. Which is just what we want him to think. Now come on . . . my horse is outside.'

11

As Thorn rode his horse swiftly under the clear stars with the girl in the saddle in front of him, she seemed to be thinking a good deal for she spoke but little. Almost two miles from the town had been covered before her mental processes took words.

'I don't quite see why you can't go straight into Ma Brendick's rooming house and arrest Jeff on a charge of murder. Tonight, for instance. You could have taken him by surprise. He'd never be expecting you.'

'He might. He's probably got a lookout posted on Ma Brendick's roof. If there was one up there he wouldn't be able to see you and me because of our distance away — but to approach Ma Brendick's would have been too big a risk. Besides, there are other considerations.'

'Such as?'

'For one thing Ma Brendick's is positively crawling with gunmen. If I got Jeff I'd never get away from the rest of them — and my job is to get them *all*. There are a lot of Twin Pines citizens included in that, who've gone over to Jeff's law-breaking. I could never single them all out individually. The thing is to let them convict themselves. All those who run into the arms of the law will automatically be arrested and roped in.'

'But, Thorn, they *won't*!' the girl protested. 'That was the original idea, I know — launching a raid on the Double-S and making all those taking part run into the law, but that will never happen now.'

'That exact scheme won't,' Thorn agreed, 'but I've worked out another one mighty like it, with just as good possibilities — and you share in it pretty largely too. I'll not go into it now: I want you to grasp it thoroughly, and riding a horse is no time to do it.'

So he gave his attention to his riding — and his surroundings in case of danger — and maintained silence until the foothills were reached. From this point onwards the trip was more or less familiar, ending at the cave where they had sheltered during their earlier getaway.

But they had not moved unobserved, in spite of their believing so. Not very far down the trail from the cave a solitary horseman drew his mount to a standstill and sat with his elbow on the saddle-horn, gazing up at the heights.

'Well, Loco,' he murmured to his horse, 'I don't reckon to know what the idea is, but I'll gamble there's somethin' comin'. Can't be too soon for me . . . '

It was not a trigger-man or one of Jeff's followers who had pursued Thorn and the girl all the way from the sheriff's office — but Joey the barkeep. That evening a chance remark dropped by Jeff in the Lucky Horseshoe had given Joey the clue that the girl was in the jail back of the sheriff's office. Joey, ever mindful for the girl's safety in the outlaws' town, had fully made up his mind to do what he could to rescue her when he had been forestalled by the arrival of Thorn. From then on he had remained watching from the shadows, following every movement — and now, it appeared, his trailing was over for the time being.

'Yeah — reckon there's no more I c'n do,' he decided. 'You an' me'd best get back to town, Loco, before — '

Joey stopped talking to himself and turned sharply as the sound of hoofs coming up the trail caught his ear. Immediately he drew his mount into the rock cover and sat watching. It was not long before a lone horseman became apparent in the starlight. By straining his eyes Joey could just make out the details of Al, Jeff's right-hand man.

Decision and action were almost simultaneous with Joey. He whipped out the gun from the holster on the saddle-bag and levelled it as he rode out of cover.

'Hold it!' he ordered. 'Stop right where you are!'

Al drew to a halt and waited, his hands upraised against the stars. Joey rode forward until he was level. He took the outlaw's guns and threw them away into the darkness.

'Goin' some place?' the barkeep asked pleasantly.

'You, huh?' Al asked sourly. 'I knew I was trailin' Tanworth and the gal an' a second horseman behind 'em, but I couldn't tell who it was — '

'Now you know,' Joey said. 'Your idea being, I suppose, to find out where they are and then dash back and tell that no-account cut-throat Jeff?'

'Try stoppin' me!' Al retorted.

'That's just what I aim to do. First time I've had the chance to catch up on one of you trigger-boys without the rest of you around for protection. Get down frum that horse!'

Al slowly obeyed, keeping his hands

up. Joey slid from his own saddle, his gun glinting in the starlight.

'All right, shoot,' Al invited. 'I can't do nothin' about it.'

'Make too much noise,' Joey responded. ''Sides, I reckon Thorn an' the gal think they've gotten away with it an' not bin followed. No reason why they should hear guns and think otherwise . . . '

'I was told to watch the north trail, an' I did it,' Al said. 'An' I'm goin' right back to report to Jeff. We've got that low-down marshal and the gal right where we need 'em — stuck in a cave which we can approach by stealth.'

Joey chuckled deeply to himself.

'What the hell are you laughin' at?' Al demanded.

'The idea of you goin' an' tellin' Jeff anythin'. Let me tell you somethin', feller. That marshal and the girl are two of the straightest shooters I ever met, an' I'm considerin' it my personal duty to protect them all I can from skunks like you . . . ' Joey suddenly reholstered his gun. 'Somethin' else you might as well know, too. I came to Twin Pines for peace an' quiet because some years ago I killed a man. He ran off with my wife, see — and because of him she died. So I figured it was right I should kill him in return.'

'What's that to do with me?' Al snapped. 'I s'pose yuh shot the guy in the belly?'

'Nope — I just broke his neck. I was a champion wrestler once — when I was younger. Comes in kinda handy sometimes — 'specially when I meet up with critters like the one who stole my wife, an' low-down murderers like you! Far as I can figger it about eight men have died from your guns. Time there was an account handed in, isn't it?'

Al started to speak again in angry protest, but he did not get the chance. Joey's right hand flashed out, seized the outlaw by the left wrist, and tugged. It was a Judo hold he exerted, for the next thing Al knew he had been flung clean over the barkeep's head and landed flat on his back in the dust. Before he could even make a move to get up Joey's knee was pressing hard in his chest and his steel-strong fingers were tightening on the outlaw's throat.

'Y'know somethin'?' Joey asked thoughtfully. 'Some folks is quite sentimental about killing folk — even when the one to be killed is a murderer several times over. Funny that, ain't it?'

'Damn you!' Al gulped, struggling vainly to free himself from the relentless hold. 'What the — the devil does it matter — to me what people are sentimental?'

'It doesn't, of course — only I thought I'd mention it, 'cos I'm not that way given myself. I know you're a killer an' that the world in general and Twin Pines in particklar will be much sweeter with yuh outa the way . . .'

Al twisted savagely and for a moment the hold weakened. Instantly he flashed up his right fist and struck Joey a killing blow in the face. It jolted him backwards and tore his hold loose. The outlaw's fist came swinging down again but Joey saw it against the stars and twisted sharply so that Al's bunched knuckles hit with tearing impact into the dust and loose-edged stones of the trail.

'Think you'll get away with it, huh?' Joey asked, and he twisted round, to reach out with both his hands. Fiercely he tugged at Al's ankles, adding a peculiar twist at the same time. With a gasp the outlaw landed flat on his face.

He kicked, struggled, beat impotently in the dust, but this time Joey took no chances. Without speaking a word he locked a forearm under the outlaw's chin and thrust a knee in the small of his back. Inevitably Al's head was forced further and further back as excruciating torment wrenched his spine.

'Joey — for God's sake!' he shrieked — and that was all. There was a sudden dull crack like the snapping of a bough before an irresistible wind and the outlaw became limp.

Slowly Joey relaxed and got to his feet, staring down at the motionless figure in the starlight.

'Nasty, but necessary,' the barkeep sighed. 'One less to bother about anyways . . . '

Stooping, he seized the body by the shirt collar and dragged it to a manzanita thicket some distance from the trail. There he dumped it. The outlaw's horse he sent scampering away after giving it one sound slap.

'If they ever find him I reckon they'll think he had a fall,' Joey mused. Then he thought a little further. 'Leastways, they will if his guns is intact.'

He went on a search for them and it took him half an hour to locate them. He put them in the dead outlaw's holsters and then stood looking up towards the mountain heights.

'Not much more I c'n do right now,' he mused. 'I'd best hop back into town and watch what Jeff does next. Mebbe I can spike his guns if need be.'

* * *

Entirely unaware of the activities of their 'guardian angel' in the lower foothills, Thorn and Claire refreshed themselves from the saddle-bag provisions and then settled down to consider the situation in more detail.

'Now, what is this plan you have in mind?' the girl asked; 'and how do I fit into it?'

'You may remember that some time ago the idea of Twin Pines being a one-ended town rather interested me,' Thorn said. 'By that, I mean that it is useful that it has only one opening — at the north, leading out to the trail.'

'Uh-huh — that's right. To the south it runs into desert. What about it?'

'Just this. What do you suppose Jeff and his gangsters would do if the town caught fire at the southern end?'

'Run for it, I suppose, like the rats they are — ' The girl paused and gripped Thorn's arm in the gloom. 'Say, just a minute. What are you getting at?'

'Thanks to you,' Thorn responded, 'the town *will* catch fire at the southern end. It will be such a sudden and unexpected affair that Jeff and his boys — and for that matter anybody else — will not have the time to turn round. They'll have only one choice — to get out quick *away* from the fire — and that means to head north. They could dodge round the back of the buildings and head south to the desert, I know, but they wouldn't without provisions because that would mean the end of 'em; and they won't have time to fix provisions, believe me. Once they hit the north trail, or at the very least *go* north, they're finished. An ambush will be there, waiting for 'em.'

'I still don't see that there is any guarantee that they *will* go north,' the girl said. 'They might scatter in all directions. Then what?'

'They'll go north if they're chasing *me*, won't they?'

Thorn could not see the girl's

startled expression, but he could sense it.

'Just a minute, Thorn! What on earth kind of risk are you proposing to take?'

'Believe it or not, Claire, this evening late on I'm going to walk into the Lucky Horseshoe, where it's pretty certain Jeff and his boys will be, and I'm going to formally charge him with murder. His reaction will be tough. I'm expecting that. I'll get scared, apparently, and make a dash for it and then head out of town to the north. Inevitably Jeff will follow me, and all those who are his followers. When they see that the fire has started — you having kindled it whilst I'm in the saloon — they'll all move out quick in pursuit of me.'

'Yes, but . . . ' The girl paused and became thoughtful, then she continued, 'Thorn, don't think I'm picking holes or anything, but what's to stop the rest of the populace of Twin Pines doing the same thing? They'll every one of them head north when they find the town on fire. How will the men in ambush know which are the gangsters and which aren't?'

'They'll know which are the trigger-men because they'll be chasing me, hell-for-leather — and also they will be the *first* to come into the picture. The other members of the town will come later. This thing's all figgered out, believe me. It relies a lot on timing, but there's no reason why it shouldn't work.'

'And you don't think Jeff and his boys will suspect a trap?'

'They may — but the chances are with things happening so fast they won't have time to think about it. Naturally, once they find what's happened there'll be a gunfight, but this time they won't get away with it because the citizens of Twin Pines will be following up in the rear, and they'll help the authorities; and in front the ambush will be so close-knit Jeff and his boys will not break through. If that doesn't tie 'em up I don't know what will. It's also the only way to sort out the guilty from the innocent.'

'In plainer language, you're just bait,' Claire said.

'Call it that.'

'Suppose some citizens stay behind to try and quell the fire? It's more than possible.'

'It doesn't matter if they do, but I think they'll realize from the very start that they won't be able to do anything. That tinder-dry pile will go up in sparks quicker'n anything once it gets lighted. Many will lose their homes and possessions, of course, but that's better than leaving Jeff in control with his murdering gang. The authorities will make it up to the homesteaders later. Isn't a great deal of value, anyways; the best stuff is out on the ranches far from the town . . . so you see,' Thorn concluded, 'a great deal is going to rely on you and me.'

'I'm more than willing,' the girl said. 'And of course I'll be able to work more or less freely because Jeff won't have the least idea where I am now I'm out of the jail.'

'Exactly. The last thing he'll expect is that you'll start a fire.'

'And once I've started it, what do I do? Run for it?'

'You'd better head northwards with the rest of the citizens. A lot of them will be walking, and you'll be doing the same. That be okay?'

'Uh-huh . . . now, about the fire,' the girl went on. 'Where do I start it?'

'At night the wind's blowing from the mountains,' Thorn said. 'Which means from the north, of course — so to blot out the southern end of the town you'll have to start about midway down the high street, then the fire will be blown southwards. The right place to start is the General Store. There'll be plenty of kerosene in that joint and once the fire gets at it, an inferno won't be in it. My guess is that the sparks from that particular blaze will easily cross the street and start the other buildings off — then the night wind will do the rest.

In less than ten minutes that whole ramshackle outlaws' town will look like something transferred from Hades.'

'Starting a fire,' the girl said, thinking, 'is not so easy as it sounds. What do I do? Just use a box of matches?'

'At the back of the General Store there are a lot of outhouses filled with old paper and straw and rubbish from packing cases. I've noticed 'em many a time. Since it will be dark when you go into action you can easily get some of that stuff and take it under the store itself. Fortunately, it's propped up on pillars like the rest of the town's buildings, to save subsidence into the sand. Make a nice little pile and light it; the dry wood will take care of everything else.'

'Which seems to cover everything,' the girl said, 'except that we have to kill time all through the day somehow.'

'That shouldn't be difficult. We'll take it in turns to sleep; and that means you sleep first. No reason why you shouldn't make a start right now.'

The girl nodded, turned back into the cave, and made herself comfortable. Thorn remained where he was at the cave entrance, gazing out over the dark expanses of foothills and the desert beyond, until at last, as he brooded like a solitary eagle, the dawn began to appear, flushing the violet sky with creeping feathers of vermilion flame.

As the light strengthened Thorn took stock of his surroundings, making certain that nobody was following up the trail. Then his brows suddenly lowered as he noticed a solitary horse perhaps half a mile away down the trail, its reins dragging as it gnawed at the few roots growing in the rocky waste.

He got up, turned back into the cave and awakened the girl. She stirred and looked at him sleepily.

'Something queer down there,' he explained. 'A riderless horse — and from the way it's behavin' there may be somebody lying out of sight near it. We could do with an extra horse for you.

I'd better go and see what's going on.'

The girl reached up and caught his arm. 'Wait a moment, Thorn! Suppose it's a trap to snare you out of hiding?'

'Mmmm — could be,' he admitted. 'Good girl; I didn't think of that. I'll use plenty of rock cover as I go down. Here's one of my guns. Use it for protection whilst I'm gone.'

The girl nodded and took the weapon from him, then, withdrawing the remaining one from its holster, he glided out of the cave and, by dodging from rock to rock, kept well out of sight. Claire watched him go, every nerve tense for a sudden shot, her mind made up that she would shoot to kill any trigger-man who fired at Thorn. But nothing happened. He reached the horse safely and the girl watched him investigating the spot. After a while he waved to her reassuringly and then started back up the acclivity, leading the horse beside her.

'We're in luck,' he told her, as at last he returned to her side. 'A spare horse

— formerly owned by Al, Jeff's right-hand man. Al himself is lying dead with a broken neck. Mebbe he fell whilst followin' us . . . mebbe lots of things,' Thorn finished, musing.

The girl looked at him, then at the horse. She shook her head.

'Al was too good a horseman to take a fall, Thorn. Sounds to me as though somebody took care of him — somebody who's on our side. Anyway, whatever the answer is, we're a horse to the good and have one less trigger-man to worry about.'

Thorn nodded and turned to the saddle-bag of his own horse at the back of the cave. From it he took some meal and thereafter spent some minutes attending to the dead trigger-man's mount. This done, he settled the animal beside his own and then set about the job of getting some breakfast for himself and the girl.

'You're leaving Al's body down there, I suppose?' Claire asked, as they ate.

'No reason why I shouldn't. He's as

good there as anywhere else, and I'm perfectly sure he doesn't rate a first-class funeral.'

The girl dropped the subject, satisfied that Thorn was right. They finished their meal mainly in silence, and then began the long wearying wait which had to carry them through the day. As on the previous occasion they could see the town of Twin Pines quite distinctly from this high eminence, and the comings and goings of the people — but nothing was clearly distinguishable. From the pervading air of peace over the place it would have been hard to realize that an infamous killer was in control.

Between times, during the day, Thorn slept whilst the girl stayed on guard. In this way, with meals at intervals, they managed to kill the hours, their interest beginning to sharpen again as the shadows of evening lengthened and the blistering sun settled at last behind the tallest ramparts of the mountains. Across the valley dark fingers stretched from the mountain peaks, engulfing Twin Pines at last. One by one the kerosene lights began to appear, gleaming fireflies in a deepening darkness.

'Who do you suppose *did* kill Al — if anybody did?' Claire asked, *a propos* of nothing.

'No idea; but there must be plenty who are for us; and whoever it was must have been following us. I don't quite know whether I like that thought or not. Anyways,' Thorn said, scrambling up from his sitting position, 'it's getting near time for us to be on our way . . . '

12

The darkness had completely settled by the time the two were on their way, and they were satisfied that they could not possibly be seen against the densely shadowed background of the mountains. As they moved, the lights of Twin Pines took on shape, resolving from dancing glimmers into the outline of lamps. Half a mile from the town's outskirts Thorn called a halt.

'We'd better part company here,' he murmured, gripping the girl's arm. 'That's the General Store there — that taller building in the middle — '

'Yes, I know,' she assented. 'I've been in the town long enough to know every part of it. What happens if something goes wrong and I'm caught? There's no guarantee I won't be.'

Thorn was silent for a moment as he reflected; then he came to a decision.

'I'd better come with you to make sure,' he said. 'Come on — and trail your horse alongside.'

Walking, the horses' hoofs making scarcely any noise in the thick grass carpet of the pasture land bordering the town, they moved silently in the direction of the rear of the main street until at last they were within a few yards of the tall wooden fence surrounding the yard of the General Store.

'Good job I did come,' Thorn commented. 'That fence will have to be scaled and the gate opened, to allow you time for a quick getaway. No job for a girl to climb that lot.'

Claire held the horses whilst he went forward quickly. For him it was no difficulty to clamber up the tall wooden palings; then he dropped silently to the other side and looked about him. The rear of the General Store, where lay the living quarters, was in darkness. Either the occupants had gone to bed or else had gone to the Lucky Horseshoe for an evening's relaxation. Whatever the answer, the coast seemed to be clear.

Satisfied, Thorn moved to the gate and drew back the bolt. The girl was dimly visible with the horses standing just beyond it.

'Tie 'em to the gate post and follow me,' Thorn breathed.

Claire obeyed and then joined Thorn as he moved to a pile of rubbish dimly visible in the starlight.

'This is what I meant,' he said. 'All kinds of old stuff — boxes, papers, straw, and what-have-you. Grab as much as you can, then come this way.'

Within a few minutes, their arms laden, they were moving across the big dark yard towards the black oblong which revealed where the space lay between the ground floor of the building and the ground itself. Throughout Twin Pines every building was perched on stilts, the only protection against the constantly moving sand foundations.

'Nothing more than this needed,' Thorn whispered, slipping a box of matches into the girl's hand. 'Give it about fifteen minutes and then set the lot on fire. After that head north as quickly as you can.'

'Okay . . . and don't run any more risks than you can help.'

'Risks are my business,' Thorn told her; then with a final encouraging grip on her arm he began to move — only to pause again. 'As things have worked out,' he said, 'you've a horse you can use for an even quicker getaway. See you again.'

He moved doubled up under the low flooring and reached the yard again, crossed it swiftly, and regained his horse. Swinging into the saddle he drew his gun, then jogged the animal down the narrow side opening between the building until he came into the main street. Everything was quiet, and completely deserted. Ominously so. With a grim face he continued on his way, stopping at last outside the Lucky Horseshoe and slipping from the saddle.

He tied the reins to the tie rack, mounted the three steps slowly, and then stepped into the saloon and stood looking about him. The pandemonium usually associated with the place died down noticeably after a moment or two, and the men and women at the tables sat looking at him blankly, then lowered their eyes to his levelled gun.

Thorn glanced over the faces sharply, as motionless as though in a photograph, then he turned his attention to Jeff. He was standing against the bar, playing with a half-filled whiskey glass, watching the proceedings intently. Joey, behind the bar, polished a bottle needlessly and glanced from one to the other.

'Well, if it ain't the marshal come back to life!' Jeff commented at last, and added cynically, 'We missed your moral support, feller.'

Thorn moved forward, his gun rock-steady. Jeff made not the slightest move, only too well aware that he would never be able to draw in time with Thorn covering him.

'One thing I like about you,' Jeff commented, with a sour grin. 'You got nerve. Remains to be seen how much good it'll do yuh.'

Thorn, mentally calculating how much time was elapsing, stopped at the bar and glanced briefly at Joey.

'Whiskey, Joey,' he said.

'Sure thing. Comin' right up.'

'Just what are you aimin' to do?' Jeff asked. 'You've gotten into the saloon, sure — but I'll bet everythin' I've got that you'll never get out. You crazy, feller?' he demanded. 'Every gun in this place is against yuh. Those that don't want t'be have no choice whilst I'm runnin' things.'

'Whilst you are,' Thorn agreed, taking the whiskey and drinking it down at a gulp so that his eyes never left Jeff's face. 'That ain't going to be for long, Jeff . . . ' And he slapped down payment for his drink on the counter.

Jeff shrugged. 'Not much that y'can do about it, fur as I can see.'

'Yes there is. I'm runnin' you in — for murder. Not just the murder of those rangers but also for the murder of my father, Sheriff Tanworth.'

'Try provin' it!'

'As far as my father's concerned it won't be difficult. I've got matching bullets — an' that's all the evidence the law needs. Since I've enough evidence to hang you for one murder I don't need to prove the other ones. You've only one neck to stretch, anyways.'

'Okay, have it your own way. Try runnin' me in, that's all!'

Thorn did not respond for a moment. He stood thinking about something, then he glanced at the barkeep.

'Joey, go take a look and see if my horse is okay,' he ordered. 'It's tied to the rack outside.'

'Sure thing . . . but why?' Joey asked in wonder.

'Never mind why. Go an' see.'

Thorn's strategy was simple enough. If the fire had started Joey would certainly see it — and say so. If not, then it was necessary to delay things . . .

Back at the General Store, however, certain unexpected happenings were taking place. Claire, judging time as best she could, remained motionless in her cramped position underneath the building's ground floor — until at last she cautiously withdrew a match from the box Thorn had given her and struck it. Its bright flame was dazzling after the darkness. Quickly she plunged it into the mass of waste paper and straw heaped up in a rough pyramid, and the blaze began instantly.

In fact, it moved more quickly than she had expected, a flame from something with a celluloid base leaping out towards her. She jumped back, forgetting for the moment that she was close to the flooring above. The impact of her head striking the woodwork made singing noises in her ears.

She scrambled forward a few yards, getting free of the choking smoke underneath the floorboards, but, as she reached the yard and tried to stand up, the full effect of the blow she had given herself took shape. She reeled dizzily and collapsed, her sense engulfed in a dark tide. Behind her the fire gained a hold, and with a crackling roar flame shot from beneath the flooring and avidly on to the wooden walls . . .

In the meantime, back at the Lucky Horseshoe, Joey was striding through the batwings in response to Thorn's order to see if his horse was okay. The barkeep reached the horse, looked it over, nodded to himself, then turned. The red glow from the back of the General Store, reaching into the violet sky, was the first thing that caught his attention.

'Fur the love o' Mike!' he breathed, and gave a gulp. 'If there ain't some trouble comin' now I'm crazy — '

He turned and floundered up the steps into the saloon again. Thorn knew the signs and smiled tautly to himself. Jeff for his part stared in wonder.

'Fire!' Joey gasped, waving his arm vaguely backwards. 'Over at th' General Store. If we don't act fast the whole town'll be ablaze.'

There was a stunned silence for a moment, then a general movement of men and women as they jumped up from the tables. But the intended rush to the batwings was halted by Thorn's voice.

'No you don't — any of you! Stay right where you are. You're not making a fire an excuse to get outa here. I came to take you, Jeff, an' I'm going to do it!'

The outlaw stood motionless for a moment, his gaze passing quickly over the hesitant men and women — then his right suddenly flashed out, not towards his own gun in its holster but towards Thorn's. Thorn could have fired, only it did not suit his policy. Instead he whipped up his gun and the outlaw knocked it sideways, delivering a left at the same time. Thorn staggered back against the bar and straightened almost immediately to meet the out-law's savage rush upon him.

'Fire, you mugs!' Jeff yelled. 'Shoot the guy while you've got the — '

Jeff did not finish his sentence, for a right to the chin knocked him spinning in a half circle. He hit the nearest table and recovered himself, and in that moment Thorn acted. Fully aware of guns being whipped out and in his direction he dived low, hurled himself through the knot of men and women, and hurtled to the batswings. Three shots followed after him and went wide.

With frantic speed he raced down the steps and to his horse. Jeff came not two paces after him, stopped just beyond the batwings on the porch and levelled his gun. Without doubt the shot would have settled Thorn's career for good, only it never landed. The figure of Joey appeared, his fists bunched. With one terrific blow he knocked Jeff clean off his feet, down the steps, and into the dusty street. How much further Joey might have gone was anybody's guess, only he did not have the opportunity. One of the trigger-men coming up behind fired relentlessly, three times. Joey lurched, staggered, and then sank to his knees — until the horde of men and women surging from the saloon knocked him over and into the dust.

Thorn did not wait to see what was happening. He dug the spurs into his horse and galloped furiously northwards away from the holocaust flaming at the opposite end of the main street. Jeff, fallen into the dirt, quickly got on to his feet again, freed his horse from the hitch-rail, and leapt into the saddle. There seemed to be no question in his mind but that he must pursue Thorn — and because he did so his fellow trigger-men did likewise. The other men and women took one look at the raging fire and discussed hastily amongst themselves. Some moved away determinedly towards the blaze with the idea of trying to quell it: the others followed on foot or on horseback in the direction Thorn had travelled.

He rode hard, glancing back over his shoulder over and over again. The sound of drumming hoofs grew upon his hearing. He slowed his pace slightly, just sufficiently to enable him to keep his distance from the pursuers. There was no question but that he could be seen. The starlight was brilliant and against the dusty chalk-white of the trail his outline was clearly distinguishable.

He kept up the pace until he reached the branching trail that led across country, then he dismounted swiftly. Immediately one of the shadows became alive and glided towards him.

'Okay, it's me,' Thorn said. 'They're following. Better be ready ... Miss Henderson arrived yet?'

'Not yet. Haven't seen a soul — 'til you rode up.'

'Queer,' Thorn muttered, frowning. 'She's got a horse to come on. Hope to heaven nothing's gone wrong.'

The ranger moved away into the darkness to pass the alert on to his colleagues. Thorn crouched down in the darkness, drawing his horse to rock cover and listening to the growing reverberation of approaching hoofs.

As they came nearer he drew his guns and waited — then as the first group of onrushing horsemen became visible he gave the order, and the ambush instantly came to life. An exchange of shots followed. Some of the men, on both sides, fell. Others, amongst the trigger-men, swerved away from the trail and hit across the pasture land. Thorn centred his attention on one of them, the recognizable figure of Jeff, and fired at him steadily. The shot missed and the outlaw went on his way at frantic pace, firing back a couple of shots as he travelled.

Thorn dived for his horse — or at least that was what he intended doing, but a hail of bullets stopped him. By the time it was safe to move again the fleeing figure of Jeff had gone. He cursed bitterly to himself and joined the circle of rangers who had closed in on the trigger-men and forced them from their horses, hands raised.

'Reckon that about takes care of 'em, Thorn,' the officer-in-charge commented.

'All but the biggest fish of the lot,' Thorn snapped. 'Jeff got away: I saw him go . . . ' He looked about him, and then in the direction of the men and women, on foot and on horseback, who were approaching. They began coming to a halt as they realized that the law was ahead of them with guns levelled.

'No sign of her here, either,' Thorn said, speaking almost to himself. 'I've got to find her — even if it means dealing with Jeff later on.'

'I can send some men after him — ' the officer-in-charge began, but Thorn cut him short.

'Leave him to me. He's my especial prize. I've got to get a confession of murder out of him. He killed my father, remember. He'll not get far anyways.'

Thorn swung into the saddle, snatched the horse's head round, and began a breakneck ride back towards Two Pines. As he went he kept passing men and women, but Claire was nowhere amongst them. His alarm deepened as the trail became empty ahead of him and the glare of the town's fire became more distinguishable, driving a backdrop of millions of sparks into the night air.

The main street was ablaze from end to end and Thorn found it necessary to detour round the backs of the buildings. Here he discovered one or two men and women doing their best — futilely — to quell the inferno, and to them he shouted as he rode up.

'Seen Claire Henderson anywheres?'

Apparently nobody had. Thorn rode on with a desperate anxiety until he came to the rear of the flaming General Store. He dropped from his horse and raced across to the still open gateway where the horse the girl had been going to use was prancing up and down nervously amidst the waves of heat.

'Claire!' Thorn called hoarsely, peering through the smoke. 'Claire! You there?'

There was no response. Shielding his face from the blaze, he hurried forward in the glare, staring ahead of him at intervals and catching glimpses of the skeletal building with the flames ruthlessly devouring its interior. Then he fell over something and fell sprawling.

'Claire!' he gasped, getting up and sweeping her limp body into his arms. 'What on earth happened — ?'

Conscious of the uselessness of speaking to her, he bore her dead weight out of the yard, then glanced back sharply as the flaming building broke in two and cascaded its raging, crackling timbers across the space he had just vacated. A queer sensation passed quickly through him as he realized that no more than ten seconds had permitted him and Claire to go on living. Nothing could survive in the holocaust that now flamed in the rear.

He released the horse the girl would have used and sent it cantering off to safety. Then he mounted his own animal and drew the unconscious girl up before him in the saddle. As he rode away from the blaze and the night air from the mountains blew about them Claire began to revive. Thorn held on to her tightly as she moved.

'What . . . happened to me?' she asked vaguely, turning her head and then rubbing the top of it tenderly.

'I reckon you ought to know about that better than me,' Thorn replied. 'I found you laid out in the yard. If I'd been only a few minutes later you'd have been dead . . . ' And he added the details as the horse thundered along, back in the direction of the northward trail.

'I hit myself on the floor . . . ' Claire made an effort at trying to remember, and then explained in full as her wits came back to her. 'Not that that matters,' she finished hurriedly, 'though I thank my lucky stars you came in time. What about the trigger-men? Did things work out right?'

'All except for Jeff,' Thorn told her grimly. 'The moment I've got you safe with the rangers I'm going to deal with him. I've a pretty good idea what's happened to him. He knows he can't get far without being nabbed — but he *has* got a chance of survival in the mountain foothills.'

'Then you're going to try and take him single-handed?'

'I've a personal score to settle, Claire. He murdered my dad, remember?'

'Then why waste time taking *me* to safety? Go straight after him and take me with you. This horse can stand it.'

'Too dangerous!'

'Dangerous be hanged. I've taken plenty of risks already, haven't I? Besides, two are more handy than one with a man as deadly as Jeff. What are you planning to do when you've captured him? Turn him in?'

'Of course: but first I want to beat a confession out of him.'

'Then you *do* need me,' Claire decided; 'if only as a witness when he starts talking.'

'Okay,' Thorn murmured. 'You win. Sure you're fit to make the ride?'

'You bet I am!'

Thorn nodded, swung the horse away from the trail, and drove it instead across the pastureland. He gave the animal free rein so that he could move at top speed — and it did, in the direction of the mountain looming nearby in the starlight. Only when the foothills came within seeing distance did Thorn slow down the pace and draw his gun from the right-hand holster in readiness. The left-hand one he slipped into the girl's fingers.

'Just in case,' he murmured over her shoulder. 'Don't stop to think if anybody looms up. Just fire. I'll take the responsibility.'

He saw her fair head nod, and the advance continued. Whether or not Jeff could see them they did not know. Certainly there was no sign of attack — until they began ascending the solitary acclivity which led upwards to the cave in which they had hidden for so many hours. Then, from somewhere not very far ahead, there came a shot. It missed the horse by about six yards, but the animal shied and halted. Quickly Thorn dropped from the saddle and lifted the girl down beside him.

'Rock cover — quick,' he breathed, pushing her forward — and he drew the horse after him as there was another revolver explosion and dust spat into the air in the starlight.

'You can't get away with it, Jeff,' Thorn called, megaphoning his hands. 'Better come out whilst you're still breathing.'

'Take more'n a single man, an' you in particklar, to get me,' Jeff's voice responded, apparently coming from the higher rocks further up the acclivity. 'If I've got to come I'm comin' the hard way — but I reckon I've a fightin' chance of gettin' away even now.'

'This is better than I'd thought,' Thorn murmured in the girl's ear. 'He doesn't know you're with me. Evidently he only saw the horse and didn't notice there were two riders. All to the good. Maybe you can draw his fire whilst I sneak round and tackle him from the back — '

'Yore mighty quiet down there!' Jeff's voice jeered. 'What's the matter? Leery? Or d'yuh know when yore licked?'

Thorn still did not answer, but to the girl he whispered, 'Let him keep on talking. I want to get an idea where his voice is coming from.'

Jeff, however, relapsed into silence at this point, so it was no longer possible to form any idea — until his revolver suddenly spat again and the echo of the explosion came back from the looming walls.

'Okay — I know whereabouts he is now,' Thorn muttered. 'Count ten and then fire the gun. Doesn't matter where so long as he hears it.'

'Right,' Claire breathed; and after

giving her an encouraging pat on the shoulder Thorn crept away in the shadows, keeping close in to rock cover. He paused after a while and waited until the girl fired the gun, then from the answering shot perhaps a quarter of a mile ahead of him he judged the outlaw's position . . . and went on again.

'If yore aimin' to make me use up my bullets, Tanworth, yore crazy!' Jeff shouted. 'I've more'n enough to take care of you . . . '

Thorn hurried his pace as the girl fired twice more and Jeff gave two answering shots. Then the vision of the outlaw himself became distinguishable to Thorn. He was half lying on a gigantic rock spur, its position such that it enabled him to see the whole of the upward trail.

Thorn smiled to himself, moved silently round the base of the spur, and then came up in the rear of it. It was not smooth. Its ragged edges afforded plenty of toe and finger hold. Thorn waited once again until there were further distant shots from Claire's gun, then he leapt swiftly up the rock as Jeff began to fire the answering shots.

Warned by the sound of Thorn's heavy boots on the rock, Jeff swung his gun round. Thorn had not time to take aim, so he did the only other thing possible. He brought the heel of his boot down on the outlaw's wrist, which, since he was lying flat on top of the rock, pinned it down hard.

'All right,' Thorn ordered; 'on your feet!'

The outlaw obeyed slowly, the fury on his face clearly visible in the starlight. His gun he was forced to drop as Thorn levelled his own weapon.

'Get down from here,' Thorn added. 'And make it quick!'

Jeff moved slowly, keeping his hands up. He was forced to turn with his face to Thorn so that he could go backwards down the rock. On the edge of it he stopped.

'How am I supposed to get down

here without usin' my hands?' he demanded.

'Simple,' Thorn responded, and leaned forward to give a shove — but in doing so he underestimated the outlaw's cunning. The instant the hand came forward, with the gun in it, he seized it and twisted it violently. Thorn fired once, blindly, then the savage twist on his arm overbalanced him and he crashed forward into Jeff. Together they fell from the top of the rock to the bottom.

Thorn was up first, just in time to land a blow in the outlaw's face since it was too close quarters to use a gun. Jeff staggered on his heels, recovered, and dropped his hands to his holsters. Before he could draw Thorn was upon him, pounding him with all the force of his massive fists.

Jeff took three blows in swift succession, then the uppercut Thorn aimed at him completely missed. Instead he took a haymaker under the jaw which dropped him to his back.

'You asked for it, feller, now you get it,' Jeff panted, dragging his guns free. 'Just try an' — '

'Drop those guns, Jeff!'

The outlaw swung round in astonishment, taken right off his guard by the sudden arrival of Claire, who had come further up the trail to investigate. She was clearly visible in the starshine, her solitary gun levelled.

'Why, you — ' Jeff made a movement to fire, but his effort was useless. Thorn, taking advantage of the diversion, brought the butt of his gun down with cracking force over the outlaw's right hand. With a yelp he dropped his gun, and the other one Thorn snatched away from him and held himself.

'Anythin' more to say?' Thorn asked coldly — then he glanced briefly at the girl. 'Thanks, Claire. Your arrival puts the situation well in hand, I guess.'

Weaponless, breathing hard, Jeff stood and glared.

'Well, what happens now?' he demanded. 'Shoot — an' get it over with. Shouldn't be too tough for you — you with two guns and the gal with one.'

'I'm not shootin' you, Jeff, much though I'd like to. The job of the law is to try you for murder. I've got the evidence of bullets that you murdered my father — but from the personal point o' view I'd like your confession of it a whole heap better.'

'Yeah? Try and get it!'

'And there's also a little matter concerning Claire Henderson here. I didn't like the way you treated her when you got her in your clutches for a while.'

'So what?'

'So this,' Thorn said quietly, putting his guns in their holsters. 'I'm going to forget that I represent the law for a moment an' become a guy who wants to square an account instead . . . get your hands up.'

'I'll be darned if I — '

Thorn's bunched fist hitting him with terrific impact in the face cut Jeff's sentence short. It was a beautiful blow, accurately timed, and it flung the outlaw on his back in the dust. He sprang up again immediately and whipped round his left. It sailed past Thorn's ear and steel-hard knuckles again found the outlaw's face. Dazed, he reeled slightly but did not overbalance.

Then Thorn really sailed into him, using coldly scientific boxing methods, all part of his training as a marshal, to hammer the outlaw into a state where he did not know what he was doing or where he was going. He finished up, blood-streaked and bewildered, with his back to the giant rock on the top of which he had earlier been lying.

'Ready to talk?' Thorn snapped.

'Like hell I will! I — '

The flat of Thorn's hand landed across the outlaw's face. He gasped a little.

'Up to you,' Thorn said. 'I can keep this up for long enough — an' if you

270

don't talk I'll really begin to take you apart . . . '

Cornered, Jeff could do nothing else.

'So I shot your old man,' he said venomously. 'So what? I was ordered to do it by Black Yankee, same as the rest of us was.'

'The difference in your case being that you *knew* you were shooting him. The others were not sure . . . You're a killer, Jeff, from beginning to end — an' you'll go the way of all killers, I guess. What about those rangers who got wiped out? You planned that too, didn't you?'

'Why not?' Jeff snarled. 'They was after me: only natural fur me to get in before 'em, wasn't it? Think I care? Like you said, I've only one neck to stretch anyways.'

'That seems to cover everything,' Thorn said quietly. 'And Miss Henderson here is a witness to what you've said. Time we started moving back. Call your horse.'

Jeff whistled briefly and his mount

came wandering into view, to pause at his side.

'In your saddle,' Thorn added, his gun in his hand again.

The outlaw obeyed: then Thorn got up behind him and kept the gun in the small of his back.

'Follow us on your own horse, Claire,' Thorn said, 'and bring mine along with you.'

'Okay . . .'

At the nudge from the gun muzzle Jeff began the journey back down the declivity. All went as Thorn wished it to until the lower reaches of the foothills were gained — then a vicious stab from Jeff's spurs sent the animal cantering wildly, stumbling amidst the stones. The outcome was inevitable. The creature tripped and fell, flinging both men headlong.

Jeff, prepared beforehand for the event, jumped up with a massive stone in his hand. Had it landed as he intended, on Thorn's head as he lay momentarily in the dust, nothing could have saved Thorn from a crushed skull — but the unexpected happened.

Claire, following with Thorn's horse, suddenly discovered that the animal had torn free of her grip on the reins. Sensing instinctively the danger to his master, he lunged forward, coming between the outlaw and Thorn at the identical moment the stone flew through the air. The animal received it in the belly, whinneyed violently, and flung his forefeet in the air. Jeff gave one frantic shout of terror as the maddened animal, fixing on him as the cause of the trouble, bore down upon him.

Thorn lay where he was, staring in fascination at the plunging horse and listening to the screams of the outlaw under the flying hoofs. Claire came up slowly on the other animal and gradually a quiet descended. The figure of the outlaw lay still in the dust, a quivering horse standing over him.

'I reckon that finishes it, Claire,' Thorn muttered, getting up and going over to her. 'Nothing to do now but send in a report ... then mebbe you an' me have got some unfinished business to attend to.'

THE END